Embroidering the Truth

A Southern Quilting Mystery, Volume 12

Elizabeth Craig

Published by Elizabeth Craig, 2020.

EMBROIDERING THE TRUTH

First edition. February 25, 2020.

Copyright © 2020 Elizabeth Craig.

ISBN: 978-1946227560

Written by Elizabeth Craig.

For Mama.

Chapter One

"For once, I'm inclined to agree with Meadow," said Beatrice.

Wyatt lifted his eyebrows and smiled at Beatrice across their small living room. "I'm almost afraid to ask what inspired that unprecedented event."

Beatrice rubbed her grandson's back. Will had finished his bottle and was sleepily cuddled up against her, his little head nestled against her neck. She breathed in the sweet baby smell of him. "He really is the best baby ever."

Wyatt walked across the room to sit next to Beatrice on the sofa. He smiled gently down at the baby. "I think you're right. I love being part of this as a grandfather. That was one of the things I'd always felt I'd missed out on—not having children."

Beatrice reached out and held Wyatt's hand. Wyatt's first wife had died before they'd had a chance to start a family.

Will lifted his head a bit and looked around. "Looks like he's not as sleepy as he was," said Wyatt. "What about a stroller ride? The weather is beautiful today."

"Good idea. And Noo-noo could use a walk, herself."

The little corgi, who'd been listening intently to them, immediately leapt to her feet upon hearing her name and *walk* mentioned in the same breath. Wyatt chuckled at Noo-noo's excitement as he put her in her harness and Beatrice carefully set Will in the stroller.

"What direction should we set out in?" asked Wyatt as they started down the driveway.

Beatrice quickly said, "*Definitely* in the direction of the church. If we head the other way, we'll be hijacked by Meadow."

"She *is* trying, though. Haven't you noticed a difference?"

Beatrice gave him a fond smile. "I've only noticed you're the very definition of an excellent pastor. You're always looking for the good in people."

"Meadow definitely seemed to realize she was dropping by too much," said Wyatt.

Beatrice watched with a smile as Will looked around him from the stroller, seemingly fascinated by the wind blowing a few dry leaves around in a miniature whirlwind. "What Meadow was doing was completely hogging Will. She was horning in on our time with the baby by coming up with any number of ridiculous reasons to drop by. I'll agree that she didn't *mean* to. But I think her epiphany had more to do with the fact that I fussed at her rather than any sudden insight on her end."

"She's been much better the last week."

"Let's see how long that lasts," said Beatrice dryly. "She must be really chomping at the bit by now to see him. After all, it's been a few hours."

They walked slowly down the sidewalk, Noo-noo stopped to smell all the apparently exotic smells along the way and Will looked around in great interest at the trees, flowers, sights and sounds around him. From time to time, Beatrice and Wyatt would stop and point something out to him—a bird or a rabbit frozen near the tree line. Will seemed completely captivated by all of it. Beatrice smiled. It was good for her ego to spend time with the baby. He appeared to think she was one of the most fascinating and knowledgeable people in the world. Plus, Will helped Beatrice look at the world with fresh eyes, just as he did.

After a few minutes, they came upon one of the oldest houses in Dappled Hills. It was a beautiful white, wooden Victorian home with turrets and delicate curlicues carved in the woodwork. The house had two circular porches: one on the bottom story, one on the top. The gardens were beautiful with camellia bushes and azaleas and pecan trees. Will was taking it all in, so Wyatt and Beatrice paused for a few minutes.

Beatrice muttered, "I sincerely hope Felton isn't lurking anywhere."

Wyatt acted as if he had no idea what she was talking about. "Felton? I think she's delightful. She was telling me the other day all about the new birdfeeders she's put up and the family of goldfinches she's feeding. She was telling me all about them. Did you know they're some of the biggest vegetarians among birds?"

Beatrice shook her head and Wyatt continued. "Apparently, they only consume insects by accident."

Beatrice snorted "Sure. You get engaging little conversations like that. That's because you tend to bring out the best in people. But I get Felton bragging about her diamond ring or the antique she's acquired or hear how hard it is to hire good help these days." She groaned. "Here she comes. She popped up out of nowhere."

Felton hurried toward them, waving as she came. She sported a colorful hat over her white hair and jaunty clothes that hung on her thin frame. She wore gardening gloves on her hands and was holding a trowel.

"Oh, let me see this darling little boy." She swooped at the stroller. To his credit, Will only blinked a few times in surprise before giving Felton a tentative, gummy smile.

Beatrice warmed up slightly to Felton as she cooed and complimented Will's cap of black curls and dimples. "I could just eat him up," she said with a sigh. "What a gorgeous baby."

"Thank you," said Beatrice with a smile. She now felt a little bad about saying such negative things about Felton just moments before. Wyatt's eyes crinkled at her.

Felton continued, "And he's lucky to have such wonderful, loving grandparents, too. Isn't it the perfect day to be outside? I couldn't resist it this morning. I had some roses to deadhead and I decided to attack them with gusto. Anyway, as I was saying, Will is fortunate to have both of you. You may know that I was raised by a series of nannies and governesses and never really spent any time with my parents or grandparents."

Beatrice stifled a sigh. Here it came. She'd felt guilty too soon.

"I suppose I can't really blame my family. My mother was married to the younger brother of a European duke and she was blue-blooded herself. That was simply the way children were raised in their social circles. Nanny would dress me up in the evenings and parade me over to see my parents for a few minutes after dinner. I would be on my best behavior," said Felton. "I'd have *loved* to see more of them and my grandparents, too. That's why I think what you're doing is so wonderful."

Wyatt, always polite, said, "You must have missed spending time with your parents. It's our pleasure to spend time with Will. He's such a cheerful little guy. And when I'm with him, I feel as if I'm seeing the world through new eyes."

Felton perked up. "I just had an idea. You should bring him around back and let him see my new feeders. The goldfinches are so beautiful that I know he'll love looking at them."

Wyatt gave Beatrice a quick sideways glance and she gave an almost imperceptible nod in response. Will would love seeing the striking gold-colored little birds and Beatrice was willing to make the temporary sacrifice of dealing with Felton in the meantime.

Wyatt carefully took Will out of his stroller and they followed Felton into her backyard. It was just like a storybook garden, matching the storybook house. There was a fountain in the middle with old brick surrounding it. The fountain area was flanked by a magnificent rose garden and beautiful gardenia bushes. The gardenias made Beatrice reflect guiltily on her whitefly problem and she vowed to find time that afternoon to mix up a soapy spray to get the issue under control.

The birdfeeders were scattered among the bushes and were all busy with chickadees, titmice, cardinals, and finches. Then Felton pointed out one particular feeder, a cylinder filled with dark seed.

"It's full of Nyjer seeds," said Felton proudly. "See how the goldfinches love the thistle?"

And indeed, the bright little birds flew to and from the feeder. Will watched them with wide eyes. They weren't too far away from the feeder, but the birds were completely absorbed in their task and not worried about their proximity a bit since they'd only known humans who helped them by setting out food and water.

Felton took off her gardening gloves to reveal a tremendous diamond ring. Beatrice had seen the ring many times before since Felton was fond of wearing it. Felton followed her gaze and held up her hand, admiring the ring, herself. "It's pretty, isn't it?"

"Very," said Beatrice in a rather dry voice.

"Family jewelry, of course. I figure I may as well enjoy them—it's not like there are many fancy occasions around here to actually wear them to. My favorite is a tiara of my mother's. It was from my father's family, naturally, since he was a blueblood."

For a second, Beatrice had thought Felton had said *bluebeard* and hid a smile. She glanced over at Wyatt and said, "Thanks so much for showing Will the feeders."

"He's loved watching the birds," added Wyatt.

Beatrice said, "But we should be heading on. We're going to go to June Bug's bakery and pick up a little treat before we walk back home."

Wyatt raised his eyebrows in surprise at this spontaneous addition to their agenda before nodding.

"Well, please do come back anytime. You don't need me to tell you where the feeders are now. He's a darling little boy and he's welcome to come see the goldfinches whenever he wants," said Felton.

They were walking away when Felton called out to Beatrice, "How is your quilting going, by the way? Are you too busy with your grandbaby to do much?"

Beatrice nodded ruefully. "I've been taking a little break. But I need to get back into it. There's a guild meeting coming up tomorrow and I'm definitely going to go. I need inspiration."

Felton said, "Same for me. Posy is actually dropping by in a few minutes to show me some of the latest fabric she has in stock. I thought that might jumpstart the process of quilting again."

A minute later, after saying their goodbyes and watching Will give an adorable bye-bye wave to Felton, they'd resumed their walk toward downtown.

"That wasn't so bad, was it?" Wyatt carefully maneuvered the stroller around a broken spot in the sidewalk.

"Wasn't it?" Beatrice sighed.

"It was kind of her to show Will the birds and to invite him back. That's a beautiful yard."

Beatrice said, "Yes, it is. But she has a lot of help, too. She has a yardman who comes at least a couple of times a week. I've seen him there when I've driven by."

"It's a big enough yard and she's an old enough lady to need some help," said Wyatt mildly.

Beatrice said impatiently, "All right, I'll admit it was nice of her. But she just can't seem to be *consistently* nice. As soon as I'm starting to think nice things about her, she starts bragging about her father, the king."

Wyatt's eyes twinkled. "I don't believe even Felton claimed he was a king."

"Well, minor European royalty or whatever. And waves her diamond ring around . . . the ring that she was wearing while *gardening*."

Wyatt slowed the stroller down as Will took particular interest in a shiny car parked on the side of the road. "She did mention that she didn't have a good occasion to wear her jewelry. It seems practical to wear it more often."

"And she has a tiara in that house somewhere. A tiara she couldn't wait to mention." Beatrice made a face.

Wyatt said, "I can't imagine your wearing a tiara even if you had one."

"True," admitted Beatrice. "I don't think it would go with my wardrobe." She glanced down at the practical khaki slacks and black button-down she was wearing for a morning of babysitting.

"I think the trip to June Bug's bakery is a stroke of genius, though," said Wyatt. "Is there anything Will can eat there?"

"Oh, he's going to have a bottle there. I don't dare mess up by introducing a potential allergen or something. But I think after a visit with Felton, you and I deserve a sweet treat."

June Bug's bakery was hopping with customers who were ordering a variety of different delicacies. Beatrice saw Will's nose wiggle as he took in the aroma of warm cakes, pastries, doughnuts, and other sweet treats. He was busy watching the people and absorbing the bright colors of the shop while Beatrice and Wyatt waited a few minutes for it to get quiet in the bakery again.

June Bug smiled shyly at them and bustled around the counter to see Will. She gently held out her finger to him and he grabbed it in his chubby baby hand.

"Better watch out," Beatrice said in a dry voice. "The next thing you know, he'll be dragging your finger into his mouth. I think he might be about to cut teeth."

June Bug beamed at her. "He's so cute." She carefully pulled her finger away and Will gave her a gummy grin.

"We're having fun with him," said Beatrice. "But I thought it might help my energy level if Wyatt and I popped by and picked up something with a little sugar. Plus, it gives us the chance to visit with you."

June Bug's eyes crinkled with pleasure.

"I was just talking with Felton Billows a few minutes ago and telling her that I really needed some quilting inspiration lately and was going to have to make it to the guild meeting. You spend so much time at the shop, I was wondering how it's affecting your own quilting." Beatrice watched as Wyatt pushed the stroller close to the display case so Will could see all the different culinary creations.

June Bug had always been very modest about her own quilting abilities. Beatrice, a former art museum curator, considered her the best self-taught quilter she knew. She had the ability to make all sorts of scraps into amazing works of original art.

June Bug said shyly, "I work on a crazy quilt when I get home. Katie and I are working on it together. Nice to spend time with her."

Katie was June Bug's elementary-school age niece. June Bug's sister had passed away and June Bug had taken care of Katie ever since.

Beatrice gave her a mock frown and teasingly said, "You were supposed to make me feel better about my lack of quilting."

June Bug's eyes twinkled. "I'm not doing *that* much every day."

The bell on the door rang and several customers came in so Beatrice and Wyatt quickly placed their orders and sat down at a table. Beatrice pulled Will out of his stroller and sat him on her lap so he could see more of the bakery. He looked curiously around as they chatted and ate their slices of cake. Beatrice was devouring a caramel cake slice and Wyatt a red velvet slice.

About fifteen minutes later, Beatrice spotted a car pulling up to the front of the bakery and made a face. "Ugh. Looks like Meadow has us on her radar somehow. Maybe she put a tracking device on Will's stroller."

Wyatt chuckled, shaking his head. "Much more likely that she needs a shot of sugar, herself. After all, we walked here, so our car isn't even out front."

And, indeed, Meadow looked surprised to see them when she pushed her way into the shop. As usual, she was wearing a riotously colorful outfit of russet reds and forest greens, which she somehow managed to pull off without clashing. She absently pushed her red glasses up her nose and headed over to their table.

"Something must be wrong," muttered Beatrice, frowning. "She hasn't even laid eyes on Will."

"Everything okay, Meadow?" asked Wyatt with concern as she approached them.

Meadow said, "That's just what I was wondering. I tried to find out from Ramsay, but he was absolutely no help at all, as usual. And Posy looked very upset."

Ramsay was Meadow's husband and the police chief for Dappled Hills. His not providing Meadow any information on what he was working on wasn't surprising, but the fact it involved Posy was. "Does this have something to do with the Patchwork Cottage?" asked Beatrice. She hoped not. Sweet Posy was one of her best friends and one of the kindest people she knew. The quilt shop was a community favorite and its warm and inviting ambiance made for an unlikely location for tragedy.

Meadow looked confused. "What? No. I mean, I don't think so. But what was Posy doing there? She seemed to have all kinds of quilting stuff with her, too. I couldn't really tell what was going on, of course. Ramsay was telling me to drive on, and in his *very firm* voice, so all I could do was to roll the window down and try and figure out what was happening from the road. And that was *not* easy."

Beatrice felt her blood pressure rising. Perhaps Wyatt was able to sense this or perhaps he could tell because of the tell-tale flush crawling up Beatrice's face. He prompted gently, "Where were you driving by? Whose house was it? Was it Posy's?"

This seemed to snap Meadow out of it. "Heavens, no. No. That's why I wasn't sure what Posy was doing there. No, it was Felton Billows's house. She's dead."

Chapter Two

Beatrice and Wyatt stared at Meadow.

"Felton?" asked Beatrice. "But we were just there a few minutes ago, on our way here. She was perfectly fine. She invited us into her back yard so Will could see the goldfinches at her new feeder."

Meadow gave a helpless shrug. "Well, she doesn't seem to be fine now, from what Ramsay was saying to me. And poor Posy."

Wyatt said, "Didn't Felton mention that Posy was going to run by the house?"

Beatrice nodded slowly. "That's right. Felton was in a rut with her quilting like I was and Posy was to come by with some quilting fabrics to inspire her and help get her back on track."

Meadow's eyes grew large. "So that's what she was doing there. Do you know what you two should do? Hand me the baby."

Beatrice said wryly, "Why am I not surprised you think that's the most important thing to do right now?"

"No, really. You should both go speak to Ramsay. You're probably the last people to see Felton alive. Maybe you can give him some information."

Beatrice said, "Or maybe it's more that you'd like to *get* some information? And Ramsay isn't being too forthcoming?"

"Maybe." Meadow reached out her arms and folded Will into them. She put her lips into the folds of his little baby neck and he gave a deep-throated chuckle. "What an adorable baby. Everyone in the shop is looking at him."

Beatrice glanced around. It seemed to her that everyone seemed very focused on their cakes and pastries. She said, "Meadow, I don't mind you taking over on the Will front, but I'm not sure Wyatt and I should go interrupt Ramsay while he's working. After all, we'll likely just be in the way."

Wyatt added, "He's probably got his hands full right now. There must be paperwork, at the least."

"And it's not as if he'll probably care what happened in Felton's final minutes, if it's a natural death." Beatrice shook her head. "It really is shocking, though. She seemed absolutely fine. *Better* than fine . . . hale and hearty. She was out in her yard deadheading roses and all."

Meadow frowned. "Didn't I say? The only thing Ramsay *did* tell me is that it was a suspicious death."

"Suspicious?" Beatrice and Wyatt stared at her. Somehow this seemed even more unlikely than a sudden medical event.

Meadow nodded. "And I don't know any more than that. The only reason I got *that* much information was because I was determined to get out of the car to speak with Posy, and Ramsay said the grounds and house were being treated as a crime scene. So you really *do* need to go over there and speak with him."

Beatrice stood up. "You're right. Here's the diaper bag. I changed the baby right before we left and he had part of a bottle ten minutes ago. We'll need to text Piper to let her know."

"I'll text her," said Meadow, waving her hand around. "Just go! And let me know what you find out."

Beatrice and Wyatt set off toward Felton's house, sans stroller this time. Beatrice said, "This is really shocking. I mean, I wasn't Felton's biggest fan, but we were just speaking with her. She was being kind to Will. And the next thing we know, she's gone."

Wyatt nodded solemnly. "Even worse, her death is suspicious."

Beatrice frowned. "Which implies someone else may have been involved. I didn't see anyone lurking around, though, did you?"

"No. Although, to be fair, I was completely focused on Will and the birds and Felton. And there were lots of trees and bushes and landscaping where someone could have hidden."

Beatrice shivered and Wyatt slid an arm around her. She said, "But surely someone wouldn't have walked up to Felton's house, lurked in her yard while she was telling us about the goldfinches, and then murdered her. That seems extraordinary. Wouldn't someone have just driven up, instead? Did you notice any cars there?"

Wyatt again shook his head and said in a rueful voice, "I wouldn't have noticed cars regardless, because it wasn't what I was focused on or concerned with. Besides, Felton's driveway is off to the side, heavily landscaped on both sides, and right next to the church's driveway where people are coming and going all the time. I don't think anyone would notice a car going down her driveway."

Beatrice said slowly, "Or someone could have parked in the church parking lot and just walked right over. There's a small path there and Felton attends church every week, so trampled it down a bit." She paused. "I mean, she *attended* church every week." They were approaching Felton's house and Beatrice saw an ambulance and a police cruiser and a white van. As they approached the property, a truck filled with yard equipment, bearing an American flag, and playing country music on high volume turned into Felton's narrow driveway.

Ramsay was in the front of the property stringing up crime scene tape. He scowled at the truck with the yard equipment, then spotted Wyatt and Beatrice and raised a hand in greeting. They saw Posy, looking shaken, sitting in the passenger seat of her car and she gave them a little wave, too.

"Don't tell me—you ran into Meadow," he said. "Actually, I *know* you ran into Meadow, because you don't have Will with you. She must have swiped him from you."

Beatrice said, "Yes, she ran into us and told us Felton had passed. And that it might be a suspicious death?"

Ramsay rolled his eyes. "And that was only minutes ago. Soon, half the town will know about it. She should go into local news."

Wyatt said, "The reason we're here is to let you know that we were speaking with Felton just forty-five minutes ago."

Now Ramsay was paying attention. He took a small notebook out of his pocket. "Were you? Could you tell me about your visit with her?"

Beatrice said, "We were just walking by with Will in the stroller. You know how he gets fascinated with things and he was staring at Felton's house and yard. She was out, deadheading the roses, and she invited us to see the goldfinches at her new thistle feeder. It was a completely ordinary conversation, which is why we're having a tough time wrapping our heads around the fact that she's gone."

"What was her demeanor like?" asked Ramsay.

Wyatt said, "Completely normal. Relaxed. She was out gardening and was excited by the fact Will was so enraptured by her yard."

Beatrice added, "It was just a regular conversation with her. She was sweet to show Will around."

Ramsay nodded, jotting down a few notes. "And you were all outside the whole time?"

"That's right. Then we left with Will to go to June Bug's for a snack," said Beatrice. She paused. "Why? Was Felton found inside?"

Ramsay sighed. "Just keep everything I tell you under your hat. She was inside the house at the bottom of the stairs. The door was wide open. Posy came over to show her some quilting fabrics and found her like that."

"How awful," murmured Beatrice. She said, "But she might have simply fallen down the stairs, right? What makes her death seem suspicious?"

Ramsay said cautiously, "That's a possibility the forensics team will keep in mind. But there were reasons for us to think there might have been a struggle at the top of the stairs. It seems probable that she was shoved down the stairs."

Wyatt's face was grim as he shook his head.

Ramsay added, "What's more, there were signs someone had been rifling through her things upstairs. It's possible a few things are missing."

Beatrice and Wyatt stared at him. "So, a break-in?"

Ramsay shrugged, "Something for us to explore. But it definitely all adds up to foul play, in my mind, anyway. I didn't know Felton Billows well. Would she have had things in the house that someone might kill to take?"

Beatrice said, "She certainly mentioned having valuable things. A tiara, for one. Felton wore that huge diamond ring, of course. She had it on even while she was gardening—I saw it when she took off her gloves."

Ramsay said in a serious tone, "She was wearing a ring when you saw her?"

"Absolutely," said Beatrice. Wyatt nodded in agreement.

Ramsay made another note. "That's interesting. She isn't wearing one now."

One of the men from the state police called out to Ramsay and he said, "I should go. I might need to get in touch with you later to ask a few more questions."

"Of course," said Wyatt. "And we won't say anything about what you've found."

Ramsay nodded. "It's fine to say she's deceased, but no details about the discovery, please." He headed off. He stopped still briefly and frowned at the middle-aged man sporting a ponytail and a five o'clock shadow who was approaching him with a weed trimmer. "Hey, you're not allowed to come through here."

"Got work to do," he said laconically.

"No, you don't. Not today," said Ramsay. He waited until the man headed toward Wyatt and Beatrice on the sidewalk.

"Devlin Harley. What's going on?" he asked as he pulled a cigarette out of his shirt pocket. He pushed it back in after Beatrice glared at it.

Wyatt quickly introduced them and said, "Unfortunately, Mrs. Billows is dead. The police are blocking off her property as part of their investigation."

He raised his eyebrows. "That so?"

"You didn't wonder what might be going on when you drove up?" asked Beatrice. She couldn't understand his lack of curiosity.

He shrugged. "None of my business, was it? Far as I figured, she might have lost something and had the cops out here to find it for her. Lots of expensive stuff in that house."

He looked so completely blasé about his employer's sudden death that Beatrice asked, "What was Mrs. Billows like to work for?"

Devlin said, "Picky. She liked everything in the yard done a particular way. After I'd mow, sometimes I'd see her out here with a pair of scissors, evening everything up."

"The yard is beautiful," said Wyatt diplomatically.

Devlin shrugged. "It's okay. It's as she wanted it."

Beatrice persisted. "I was wondering . . . you don't seem surprised or very concerned about her death."

"It happens, doesn't it? Whether we want it to happen or not. My mama always says it's always sneaking up behind us and we'd better live each day like it's our last."

Beatrice felt a cold shiver go up her back. Devlin's mama had an eerie way of putting things.

Devlin continued, "Plus, Mrs. Billows wasn't the greatest at paying people. Ask anybody."

"Did she have other folks working for her?" asked Beatrice.

Devlin nodded. "Sure. Got that kid running errands for her so she didn't have to go out in her car. She was a menace out on the road in that car of hers. Her and that other old lady were always driving up on the sidewalks."

Beatrice and Wyatt glanced at each other. Devlin was most likely referring to their friend, Miss Sissy. Miss Sissy seemed to believe the sidewalks were an important part of the roads . . . perhaps a turn lane . . . and shook her fist at pedestrians who tread on them.

Beatrice asked, "Mrs. Billows didn't pay him, either? The kid running errands?"

"Nope. And she was weeks behind paying me. She told me she was definitely going to pay me my back wages today, along with today's pay." He made a face. "Guess that ain't going to happen anytime soon."

Beatrice asked, "Did she give any excuses about why she was behind on paying you?" She glanced around again at the big house and nice yard and remembered the fancy car that Felton apparently rarely drove.

"She acted like she was out of checks and had forgotten to ask the kid to cash a check at the bank. But I bet you anything it's because she didn't have that money. It wasn't that she was cheap, it's that she was broke. I can recognize broke, right? I told her she should cash in that diamond ring she was always flashing around. Bet that would pay for a few weeks of grass-cutting."

Wyatt asked, "What did she say in response to that?"

Devlin snorted. "Just about snapped my head off, that's what. Said she *had* the money, just not on her and she wasn't going to go around selling her family's jewelry and such. I told her she'd better think of something or else she wasn't going to have any help over here at all and it's a big house." He stared thoughtfully at them for a moment. "You don't reckon her death wasn't completely natural, do you? That it wasn't really her time?"

"What makes you wonder that?" asked Wyatt.

"No real reason. Just that sometimes she made folks upset with her." The one spark of curiosity was suddenly extinguished and he once again seemed remarkably blasé about his employer's demise. "Like that Haskell kid. Whatever his name is. He's a slick kid. Hard as nails, but whenever the old lady was around, he'd always be real polite and friendly. He was a favorite of hers, but I can't stand him. And believe me—he's not all sweetness and light. I've seen him on the wrong side of town with the wrong sort of people."

Beatrice frowned. "There's a wrong side of Dappled Hills?"

He gave her an exasperated look. "As if. No, the wrong side of Lenoir. I go there sometimes to see a friend of mine. I've seen that kid there and he's with a bad crowd, let me tell you." He looked curiously at Wyatt. "So, you're a preacher, that right?"

Wyatt smiled at him. "That's right. At the church right next door, actually."

"Is that right?" he paused. "I been thinking about going back to church. Mama goes to this other church, but it never felt right to me, so I haven't been for ages."

"You're always welcome at Dappled Hills Presbyterian."

Devlin continued, "I've never been too religious. I might not know what to say at the right part of the service."

Wyatt said, "Everybody is welcome to come—you don't have to consider yourself very religious. You can visit and see if you like it there."

Beatrice added, "And there's no way you can mess up. It's completely foolproof . . . the bulletin has all the words for the service on it."

Devlin looked pleased. "Okay. So when do you have service? I mean, I know on Sunday and everything. But when?"

"We have an eight o'clock service and an eleven o'clock," answered Wyatt.

"Don't think I'll get up early enough for the eight, but the eleven might be doable," said Devlin slowly.

Wyatt smiled warmly at him again. "I'll be sure to keep an eye out for you to welcome you."

Chapter Three

A few minutes later, Beatrice and Wyatt were walking back to their house. Beatrice said, "I still have a hard time wrapping my head around the fact that Felton is gone. I mean, we were just *there*. If it wasn't a natural death, someone must really have been quick about it." She looked at Wyatt. "I don't feel as if I knew Felton well, since I was always trying to avoid her whenever I saw her coming. What do you know about her?"

Wyatt said thoughtfully, "Well, she had a real eye for detail. She was very particular about how she dressed and what her yard and house looked like. I think she liked things organized, from what I remember of her time on a church committee."

"Who were her friends?" asked Beatrice. "I know she was a quilter, but she apparently didn't join a guild. Or, if she did, she must have dropped out."

"Posy could probably answer your questions about her quilting," said Wyatt.

Beatrice put her hands over her mouth. "Posy! I completely forgot about poor Posy with talking to Devlin."

"But you couldn't speak with her—Ramsay and the state police were still having a conversation with her," said Wyatt.

"Just the same, I'm going to head back. Sorry, Wyatt."

Wyatt said, "No—you're a good friend. See to Posy."

When Beatrice returned to Felton's house, she saw Posy was just finishing up giving her account to a state policeman. Her little friend was teary-eyed and looked relieved when she spotted Beatrice there.

Posy walked over and Beatrice gave her a hug. "Are you all right?"

Posy quickly blinked a few times and nodded. "I think so. But poor Felton."

She definitely looked rattled and her gaze was drawn to the police bustling in and out. Beatrice said, "Do you want to go somewhere else? My house, maybe? Or to get something to eat?"

Posy nodded again. "Could we go to my house? I have sandwich stuff we can both eat. And Amy is taking care of the shop this afternoon."

"Of course we can. Did you drive here?"

Posy looked worried. "I did—my car is in the driveway. But I don't think it's a good idea for me to do any driving right now. I'm a little shaky."

"I'll drive your car. And Wyatt can pick me up in a little while from your house." Beatrice reached out and gave Posy another quick hug.

A few minutes later, Beatrice pulled the car into Posy's driveway. Beatrice had always loved Posy's house. The front yard was blanketed by flowers in a sort of English garden effect. Rimming the little house were flowering bushes of all sorts. And there were birdfeeders and birdhouses in cheerful colors that Posy's husband, Cork, had made.

Posy had been quiet on the way over and Beatrice had respected that and let her have some time with her thoughts during the short drive. But now, she was wondering if Posy might need a distraction. Beatrice made light talk about various cute things Will had done recently, tempting a small smile out of Posy a couple of times.

They sat down at Posy's weathered kitchen table and Posy said, "Beatrice, I really appreciate you. Thanks so much for coming to get me and bringing me home."

"I was happy to do it," said Beatrice firmly.

Posy smiled at her and said, "I think it was just that it was such a surprise. Do you mind if we talk about it a little? I think it might help me work it all out in my head."

"Of course we can," said Beatrice.

Posy took a deep breath. "Felton had been having a little bit of a dry spell with her quilting. I think you were telling me that you're having the same thing?"

Beatrice nodded. "I've been busy with the baby and the whole new-grandma thing. And I suppose I made so many small projects before Will was born that maybe I got a little burned out. But I'm making it to the next guild meeting for inspiration."

Posy said, "Exactly—inspiration. That's why I suggested to Felton that I bring by different fabrics so she could take a look. Sometimes when you look at a piece of fabric, you can suddenly visualize the whole project. You can see what it *could* be."

"I heard that Felton wasn't doing a lot of driving. I'm guessing that's why you offered to run by?"

Posy said, "Yes. She has a boy who runs errands for her, but I thought it might be better if I brought the fabrics by myself so I could sort of *present* them."

She was looking like she might be absorbed by her thoughts again and Beatrice said in a gentle voice, "You know, Wyatt and I were with Felton just a few minutes before you arrived."

Posy's eyes grew wide. "Really?"

Beatrice nodded. "We had Will with us in his stroller and Felton wanted to show him the goldfinches in her garden. Felton even mentioned that you were going to be coming by. She sounded very grateful."

This made Posy's eyes glisten with tears. "Oh, thanks for telling me that, Beatrice. I'm so glad she was looking forward to getting back into quilting. I'm just sorry that she never got the chance. And Ramsay seemed to think she hadn't had a natural death." She shook her head. "I just can't believe it. Who would do such a thing?"

Beatrice said, "I'm sure Ramsay will get to the bottom of it. I'm so sorry this happened to you, Posy. Do you want me to call Cork?"

She shook her head. "No, he's working and I don't think he has backup today for the store. I'd hate for him to have to close up. I'll be all right. It's just the shock. You see, I walked up to Felton's door with all my fabrics. The door was ajar. I put the fabrics down on the front porch and rang the doorbell, which I could hear through the house because the door was open. I thought Felton would maybe call out to me and tell me she was on her way, but it was completely silent."

"That must have been very eerie," said Beatrice.

Posy took another deep breath. "It was. I thought maybe she was in the bathroom or something, but I was exactly on time and you know Felton appreciates punctuality. So I hesitantly pushed the door open farther and called her name. That's when I saw her at the bottom of the stairs." Posy shivered.

Beatrice stood up from the kitchen table and found the closest quilt—a well-worn and obviously loved cheerful pinwheel pattern—draped over the back of the sofa and gently put it around Posy's shoulders.

Posy gave her a grateful smile. Then she said slowly, "I could tell right away that she was gone, the poor thing. Her eyes were wide open and staring at me. It was just terrible. Those stairs of hers are so steep and I figured she must have taken a tumble. Accidentally missed a step or something. Of course, I called Ramsay right away and backed out of the house. I sat down on Felton's front steps because I felt like my knees were going to give away."

She shook her head abruptly as if trying to rid her mind of the images there. "I'm so sorry. Let me get something for us to eat and drink."

Beatrice stood up. "No, let *me* get something for you to eat, Posy. Please. You've had a terrible shock. Besides, I've just had cake at June Bug's. Can I make you a sandwich?"

Posy looked a little anxious at being a bad hostess and Beatrice quickly added, "And I'll pour myself a glass of water."

A few minutes later, Beatrice had a sandwich, chips, and a drink for Posy and a glass of water for herself. She sensed Posy was finished talking about Felton and she spent a few minutes chatting some more—this time about things going on at the church and the upcoming guild meeting until the color came back into Posy's cheeks and the sparkle to her eyes.

Posy reached out and gave her hand a squeeze. "Thanks so much, Beatrice. You've been such a good friend. I think I'll be all right now. I know you must have things to do."

"Are you sure you don't want me to call Cork?"

"No, thanks. I might take a little nap. That will likely make me feel better. Can I drive you back home?" asked Posy.

"Wyatt will come pick me up. But I'm going to start walking in the direction of home—I think a real walk might do me good. Stroller rides with Will and walks with Noo-noo don't really count . . . they're way too slow for real exercise."

Posy said, "Give that baby a hug for me and Noo-noo a rub. And thank you again, Beatrice."

It wasn't long before Wyatt pulled over next to her on the side of the road, looking at her with concern in his kind face. She hopped into the car for the short ride home.

"How is Posy holding up?" he asked.

"She'll be fine, although it was all a terrible shock for her. She had something to eat and drink and said she was going to take a nap. Hopefully, she'll feel a bit better after that."

Wyatt nodded and pulled into the driveway. As they were walking into the house, his phone rang. He answered it and frowned as the caller spoke. "Yes, I'm home now, Betty. You're wanting to come by?" He glanced up with an inquiring look for Beatrice and she nodded her head. "You're welcome to come by. See you in a few."

After he hung up, Beatrice said, "Was that Betty Lamar?"

He said slowly, "It was. She sounded like she was upset, too."

Beatrice ordinarily wasn't too much of a fan of members of the congregation popping by their house, but Betty was something of a special case. She was an incredibly helpful church member who volunteered for nearly every committee and mission project. Plus, she was one of those members who preferred to stay in the background, never aggrandizing or calling attention to herself or her constant work for the church. And she'd never come by the house, not once.

Betty soon arrived, sending Noo-noo into a surprised yelping until she came in and rubbed her tummy.

"Can I get you something to drink or a snack?" asked Beatrice.

Betty stood up from rubbing the corgi and flushed a little. "Oh, no. Goodness, don't worry about me. Just thanks for letting me run by like this."

Beatrice smiled at her. "I'll let you two talk, then." She started walking toward the bedroom.

"Oh, please don't go, Beatrice. I'm interested in hearing your thoughts, too," said Betty.

"Would you like to come sit down?" asked Wyatt politely. They walked into the small living room area and sat down on the sofa and armchairs there.

Betty flushed again. "You know how quickly news travels in a small town. I heard about Mrs. Billows a few minutes ago."

To his credit, Wyatt looked only slightly surprised at the topic. He was likely expecting Betty to either bring up a personal problem or a church-related concern. He said solemnly, "We were sorry to hear the news, too. Were you friends?"

Beatrice was remembering the yardman told them Betty's son was Felton's errand-runner, to help keep Felton from having to drive.

Betty quickly said, "No, not like that. Really just acquaintances. You see, my son ran errands for her a few times a week after school. You know, he'd drive to the grocery store or the drugstore or the post office. He liked doing it, too. They really got along."

But the hurried way she said it made Beatrice think that perhaps there was something else she wasn't mentioning. Devlin, the yardman, had seemed to think that Haskell ran with a bad crowd.

Wyatt said, "I'm sure she must really have appreciated his help."

Betty nodded eagerly. "She did. She was a terrible driver and was trying to stay off the roads. Sometimes Haskell would even drive her car for her, just to keep it in good shape since it was in disuse."

"That was very kind of him," said Wyatt.

Betty hesitated. "Well, he was also being paid, of course. That was when Mrs. Billows remembered. Haskell would sometimes be a little grumpy when he came home and she'd forgotten again. But I told him that older folks sometimes had a hard time remembering things—that it's easy for stuff like that to fall through the cracks,"

Beatrice raised her eyebrows. Felton Billows had been as sharp as a tack. Nothing escaped her notice. The yard alone showed her eye for detail. If she hadn't paid Haskell or Devlin, it certainly wasn't because she'd forgotten.

"Anyway," said Betty in a rush, "I wanted to hear more about what happened. I want to make sure to give Haskell the truth, but not make it too awful. I think he'll be really upset when he hears. He was quite fond of Mrs. Billows."

Wyatt gave a careful account of the little they knew, leaving out anything Ramsay hadn't wanted them to mention, while Betty hung on every word, frowning.

"So . . . it was just a terrible accident then?" Betty's face lit up with relief.

Beatrice thought this was an odd reaction. Had Betty thought that Felton might have been a victim of foul play?

Beatrice said, "The police aren't certain, so they're investigating."

The worried line appeared again between Betty's eyebrows. "Oh. I see. So it's one of those things where they really can't tell."

"I think it's one of those things where they're simply covering all the bases," said Beatrice.

"I do hate to tell Haskell about it. He'll feel terrible that he wasn't there to help her or look out for her." She looked shyly at Wyatt. "Do you think you could do me a favor? Both of you, actually."

"Of course," said Wyatt and Beatrice together.

"Haskell will be at youth group tonight, of course. Do you think you could say a few words to him? Something encouraging, maybe? Or maybe just that you think Mrs. Billows couldn't have suffered much. She couldn't, could she have?" Betty suddenly looked anxious.

"I'm sure she didn't," said Beatrice in a comforting voice. And she couldn't have, after all. Posy must have arrived at Felton's house only minutes after Beatrice and Wyatt left.

"We'll be sure to have a quick word with him," added Wyatt.

"Thank you," said Betty simply. "You just don't know how much I appreciate that. He may not look it, but he's a very sensitive boy. Things tend to hit him hard and he covers it up with sort of a blustering manner. He'll seem very brash sometimes, but that's because he's always carrying so many feelings along with him. I really do appreciate it." She stood up from the sofa. "And now, I really must be on my way and leave you two to the rest of your afternoon. Thanks again."

By the time Wyatt and Beatrice had risen to their feet, she'd already slipped out the door.

"What did you make of that?" asked Beatrice, looking thoughtfully at Wyatt.

He sighed. "I'm not sure. I'm glad she tacked on that addendum about how she considers Haskell sensitive. I wouldn't have understood it, otherwise."

Beatrice nodded. "Honestly, I'm trying to place him. So many of the boys in youth group tend to run together; I know that's awful of me to say. They all seem to have long hair, baggy clothes, and wear athletic shorts all year round."

Wyatt said, "Haskell would actually be one of the ones who smiles at adults when he sees them."

Beatrice raised her eyebrows. "That's nice. And not something I've witnessed a lot of with the boys."

Wyatt hesitated. "This isn't particularly nice for me to say, but I always wondered if it was genuine."

"I think it's completely understandable for you to wonder that. After all, the yardman, Devlin, seemed to think Haskell was buttering Felton up. And he mentioned Haskell was involved with a rough crowd."

Wyatt said, "I'm not quite sure what to make of it all, but I'll definitely have that conversation with Haskell later . . . did you want to be there, as well, as Betty suggested?"

"I suppose so, although I'm not really sure what good I can do."

Wyatt's eyes twinkled. "I don't know—I think you have a good rapport with teens. At least, that's what I've noticed."

Beatrice snorted. "Maybe because I'm no-nonsense? Because I cut to the chase? It's not as if I'm the Teen Whisperer or anything." She paused. "This has all taken your day on a detour, hasn't it? We were just going to have a simple walk and then you were going to get some work done."

Wyatt looked at his watch. "True, but that's sort of a typical minister's day. Lots of detours. It's all right, I'll just get started on my sermon notes now."

The doorbell rang and Wyatt and Beatrice stared at each other.

"Grand Central Station," murmured Beatrice as she walked to the door amid Noo-noo's barks.

Chapter Four

I t was Piper, peering at her with concern. "Is everything all right?" she asked as she followed Beatrice inside.

Beatrice frowned. "If Meadow didn't give you the message that she's got Will, I will absolutely string her up."

Piper said, "Don't. She delivered it. But she told me what happened and I wanted to run by and make sure you were both all right. That must have been a real shock, having seen Mrs. Billows and then having her pass away like that."

Wyatt said, "It was really tough for both of us to wrap our heads around since we'd just seen her. She was being very kind and showed Will her goldfinches. But we're all right. Piper, I hope it's all right, but I was just about to leave to head for the church and get some work done in my office."

"Of course," she said. "You're probably really off-schedule, with everything that's happened."

As Wyatt walked out, Beatrice said, "Do you want something to drink? Or a snack?"

Piper shook her head as she plopped down on the sofa. "No thanks. I've got to get Will from Meadow, so I only have a few minutes."

Beatrice said wryly, "I'm sure you could have a great many more than that, if you wanted. It's not as if Meadow is counting down the seconds until you come to retrieve the baby. She looked delighted to be taking him off my hands earlier."

Piper chuckled. "Well, that's true. I guess it's more that *I* want to spend more time with him now that I'm done with work."

"How is it going there?" asked Beatrice. "It's got to be a very different type of day."

After Will was born, Piper had decided to work at the elementary school part-time—and in the office instead of in the classroom. The school needed someone to do accounting and it was for only a few hours a day. It worked out well for everyone because Beatrice and Meadow helped watch Will a couple of days and then he was in the church's nursery program for the others.

"It's good," said Piper. "But I really miss the kids. When they come into the front office, they just light up when they see me and call out my name. But the part-time work really suits me for right now; I couldn't stand to be away from Will longer than I already am. When he gets a little older, though, I'll probably go back to teaching. Now enough about me; I came over to find out about *you*. And Wyatt. What on earth happened? Meadow left me some sort of garbled message on my phone and didn't answer me when I called her back."

Beatrice said, "She's probably playing with Will in the sandbox or something. You know how she gets completely focused to the exclusion of everything else. But to answer your question, Wyatt and I are absolutely fine. It was just a jolt, as Wyatt was saying earlier. We'd walked by her house a few minutes before, with Will in his stroller. She'd shown us her backyard. Then we were at June Bug's bakery having a snack and Meadow came in with the news."

Piper said, "And you went by Felton's house again? Is that what Meadow was saying?"

"We did, only briefly. Poor Posy was there and she was pretty shaken up. One of the things that had come up in our conversation with Felton was that Posy was coming by to bring some fabric samples for Felton to see. She was hoping they'd inspire her to jump back into quilting. So Posy ran by the house, saw the door ajar, and then found Felton."

Piper winced. "That's so awful for her. Is Posy all right?"

"She is. I drove her back home and made sure she had something to eat. She hadn't eaten, apparently, and I don't think that helped. She was looking pretty pale for a while."

Piper said slowly, "And it was an accident? Or not?"

"Who knows? Ramsay and the state police are investigating now to see what they can find out." But she remembered Ramsay stating that jewelry might be missing.

"If it was murder, I just can't figure who would do such a thing," said Piper. She added, "I mean, I know Mrs. Billows sometimes was a little annoying. But no one kills someone because they're annoying. She was pretty innocuous aside from that."

"Aside from the bragging, you mean? I suppose she was. The bragging *was* pretty outrageous, though."

"Was it all true?" asked Piper curiously.

"Maybe. I don't know. Meadow said Felton's family had been in Dappled Hills for a long time. I suppose, anyway, that her *mother's* family had been here for a while. Her father was supposed to be European or something, I gather." Beatrice frowned. "There was one other thing. Both Felton's yardman and her teenage errand-runner apparently have reported Felton hadn't paid them."

Piper raised her eyebrows. "Really? That seems kind of weird. Mrs. Billows always seemed to have plenty of money. Did she just forget?"

"That's what Betty Lamar said, or at least what she told her son. But Devlin, Felton's yardman, was pretty bent out of shape over it."

"You don't think that either of them could have killed Mrs. Billows because she hadn't paid them, do you?"

Beatrice said, "If she *was* murdered, I didn't get the impression it had been part of some elaborate plan. Maybe one of them arrived at the house, asked Felton for money, and then became furious when she wouldn't pay up. It could have been something completely spontaneous. Perhaps they asked for wages, Felton deliberately walked upstairs to avoid them, and they followed her up, continuing to argue."

"Well, it definitely doesn't sound like a great way to get back wages," said Piper.

Beatrice said in a thoughtful voice, "The yardman arrived pretty quickly on the scene and didn't seem at all surprised about the emergency vehicles there. It makes me wonder. Maybe he murdered Felton, drove off, and then made a show of arriving back at the house in front of the police and everyone."

"How did he seem?"

Beatrice said, "He wasn't worried about Felton at all. He didn't ask any questions. For all intents and purposes, he'd arrived to take care of the yard and he was planning on proceeding with the task."

Piper sighed. "That's all so odd. Well, I guess Ramsay is on the case, though, and he'll have gotten to the bottom of it all."

Beatrice felt as though Piper's words were just the slightest bit pointed—stating she didn't want her mother trying to figure out what had happened. She gave Piper a reassuring smile.

Piper stood up. "Well, anyway, I'm glad that you and Wyatt are all right. I'm going to head over to Meadow's now. Let me know if you hear anything else."

"Will do," said Beatrice as she walked Piper to the door.

The rest of the afternoon passed quietly with Wyatt at the church office and Beatrice and Noo-noo left to their own devices in the cottage. For once, Beatrice didn't have the restless feeling propelling her to do anything other than relax. She picked up the novel she was reading and headed to the backyard with Noo-noo in tow. Beatrice had always loved her backyard, even though it wasn't nearly as grand as Felton's was. She also had some birdfeeders and birdhouses, courtesy of Posy and Cork. The yard itself was very private, bordered with flowering bushes and scattered with different trees. And there was lots of shade so it never got too stifling hot

Fully intending to read, she climbed into the hammock. A minute later, she'd fallen asleep.

She'd slept so deeply that when she woke up, she wasn't sure where she was. She blinked up at the canopy of trees above her and then remembered the hammock. Beatrice glanced down to see Noo-noo looking reproachfully up at her. Sometimes Noo-noo cuddled with Beatrice in the hammock, but this time Beatrice had fallen asleep before she'd invited the little dog up with her.

She looked at her watch and groaned. There was a load of laundry she'd planned to take care of before she met up with Wyatt at church that evening. There was also supper to be made . . . unless she and Wyatt grabbed some food at youth group. As late as it was, she was already thinking of ways to cut corners.

She made the laundry a small load to run it faster, then fed Noo-noo. Then she quickly went through the list she'd originally planned on completing before falling asleep. When Wyatt came in to change before heading back out to youth group, Beatrice was pushing the vacuum around and yelped in surprise when she spotted him.

Beatrice turned the vacuum off.

"Sorry," said Wyatt ruefully. "After the day we've had, no wonder you startled. You've been very productive, I see."

Beatrice snorted. "Appearances can be deceiving. This is me scrambling after taking a monster nap in the hammock. I hope you managed to get more done than I did."

Wyatt chuckled. "As a matter of fact, I fell asleep in the office, myself. But I only nodded off for a few minutes, so I managed to get the sermon done, some emails sent, and some other work I needed to knock out."

"Glad one of us got everything finished. I didn't even start supper—do you think we could just grab something at youth group? What are they eating tonight?"

Wyatt opened his phone to look at the church calendar online. With the church secretary, Edgenora, in charge, the church calendar had changed to an amazingly organized entity with all sorts of information included. Beatrice still remembered all the random phone calls both she and Wyatt had gotten in the past from church members looking for information. Now, they could simply check online. Some of the older members still preferred making a phone call, but now they could call the church office and Edgenora could give them what they needed. This fact made Beatrice very happy.

"It looks as if they're eating tacos," said Wyatt.

"That sounds pretty good. It's either that or sandwiches here before we run out." Beatrice looked down at herself. "And I need to change, too."

"You really look fine," said Wyatt.

"Thanks for that. You aren't seeing all the spots on my clothes, though. I think Will must have spat up a little on my shoulder."

Miraculously, they were both ready and changed and at the church right before everyone started arriving for youth group. The program was one of the biggest successes at the church. The youth minister was young herself and excellent at making youth group fun. It's an age-group that can be very awkward in groups, but the youth minister had managed to keep it from being that way and the kids all seemed to be friends with each other.

"Now which one's Haskell?" murmured Beatrice, glancing around.

"The one walking over to us," said Wyatt. "Like I said, he's a friendly kid."

After a couple of minutes speaking with Haskell, Beatrice decided that he was more of an *obsequious* kid. He was definitely nice, but the niceness rang a little hollow somehow. It just seemed a bit over-the-top. Fake. She chided herself for feeling that way, but that's the way she felt. He was clean-cut, despite his shaggy hair. Whatever "bad crowd" he was hanging around with, it was doubtful it was from youth group. She could tell they looked up to him and he functioned as sort of a leader among the boys.

Haskell said, "I did want to come talk to you both for a reason. I heard that you were at the house right after Mrs. Billows was found."

Wyatt nodded solemnly. "That's right. I understand you worked for her."

"I ran errands for her around town so she wouldn't have to drive. Mom said I was saving the town from a terrible fate." He shook his head. "I never actually saw her drive, so I couldn't say. But I feel real bad for her. I wish I'd been there so I could have kept it from happening. I wasn't even doing anything—just hanging out at home with my mom."

Wyatt said, "You shouldn't feel bad about not being there. There was nothing you could have done. And I don't think she could have suffered at all. She was found very quickly."

Haskell said, "Do you know if her death was an accident? Or . . . not?"

Wyatt paused. "I think the police are trying to figure that out. They're investigating."

Haskell said, "Well, it just seems like if I'd been there I could have kept her from falling, you know. She could have held onto my arm. And, if it wasn't an accident, maybe I could have scared off whoever did this to her."

Beatrice frowned. "Why do you think she had a fall?"

Haskell gave a small shrug and smile. "What else could it have been? She was an older lady. Even though she was really stable on her feet, things happen. I guess she fell on that big staircase of hers. She was always over-confident about what she could do. I kept taking things out of her arms—stuff she thought wasn't too heavy. Maybe she was carrying a bunch of things on the stairs and fell down. Seems likely."

Beatrice and Wyatt didn't answer this right away and Haskell continued, "Anyway, I hated to hear it happened. Mrs. Billows and I got along really well. If I find out it *wasn't* an accident, then I'm going after whoever did it."

Beatrice asked, "Why do you think someone might have done such a thing?"

"Money," said Haskell simply. "She had money, right? And she had a lot of nice things in her house . . . jewelry and antiques and silver and stuff. I guess somebody thought she'd be easy to steal from."

"Would she have been?" asked Beatrice.

"Definitely. She talked a lot about the stuff she had because she was proud of it. She was proud of her family and the house and the whole thing. Plus, she kept her door unlocked all the time. Said that was one of the benefits of living in a small town—that you didn't have to worry about people breaking in."

"But it's not a break-in if you leave the door unlocked," said Beatrice.

"Right. But taking stuff is. I bet I know who did it, too, if somebody killed her," said Haskell darkly.

"Who?" asked Beatrice and Wyatt simultaneously.

"That yard guy of hers. Devlin."

Beatrice raised her eyebrows. Those two must not like each other much. Devlin had implicated Haskell and now Haskell was implicating Devlin.

"What makes you think that?" asked Beatrice.

Haskell shrugged again. "Just the way he was with her. I mean, I'm still a kid but I know you're supposed to be nice to people who employ you. Right?"

"And he wasn't?" asked Wyatt.

"Nope. He was real gruff with her all the time and acted like he knew what he was doing more than she did. Which is crazy! I mean, did you ever look at her garden? It's obvious she knew what she was talking about when it came to her yard. But he'd correct her all the time or argue with her about something she wanted him to do in the yard. Then he had this *big* argument with her just a few days ago."

"What were they arguing about?" asked Beatrice.

"Money," answered Haskell again. "See the pattern?"

Beatrice said, "Your mom said maybe Mrs. Billows wasn't great about paying on time?"

Haskell said, "Oh, you know—she'd forget sometimes. Or she'd wait until she had cash so she didn't have to write me a check. Save me the trouble of having to go to the bank. It was fine for me, but I guess Devlin wasn't too happy about it." His eyes had a slightly malicious gleam before his expression went back to neutral.

"You seem like you know a lot about what was going on there," said Beatrice. "Was there anyone else who spent a good deal of time at the house? Somebody who might be aware of the kinds of things she had at her house?"

Haskell said, "Like I mentioned, *everybody* knew the kinds of things she had at her house because she'd talk about them. But if you mean who her friends were and stuff, she mostly hung out with her friend Edith. Or, anyway, she'd talk about Edith a lot."

Wyatt asked, "Is that Edith Fairchild?"

Haskell said, "I don't know her last name, but there couldn't be too many Ediths, right? Not in a small town like this."

"What's she like?" asked Beatrice. "I don't think I know her."

"Hopeless," said Haskell with a laugh. "Totally scatter-brained. Kind of silly. But they got along really well. Maybe she knows more about what might have happened to Mrs. Billows." He looked back over at his friends and said, "Anyway, thanks for talking to me about it. I wanted to talk to somebody who was there today." He quickly walked off to join the other kids.

Beatrice and Wyatt headed over to the buffet line to pick up some food. Wyatt said quietly, "I'm not sure if our conversation with him actually did any good."

"I'm not sure if he was all that upset," said Beatrice. "I'd gotten the impression from his mother that we'd maybe offer some sort of comfort to Haskell. But I think he mostly wanted to speak with us to find out more information about what happened."

Wyatt nodded. "Exactly. I would have said more, maybe even led us in a prayer, but I don't think that's what he was looking for."

Beatrice nodded. "I think that's all he needed."

They got their food and sat down at a table near the kids. Beatrice frowned as Wyatt's phone rang. "It's the day that won't end," she murmured.

Chapter Five

He pulled it out of his pocket and answered it. He listened intently for a couple of minutes and then said in a comforting voice, "I'm so sorry. That must have been a terrible shock. Of course you can come by." He quirked a questioning eyebrow at Beatrice, who suppressed a sigh and nodded. The day that wouldn't end apparently would go on a bit longer. "I'm eating at the church right now, so can we say forty-five minutes? All right. See you then."

"Everything okay?" asked Beatrice.

Wyatt shook his head and said quietly, "That was Edith Fairchild. She's definitely the Edith who was Felton's good friend. She's very distraught and asked if she could come by the house."

They ate their Mexican food, Wyatt led the youth group in a prayer to start out their evening, he spoke with a couple of the kids, and then he and Beatrice hurried back home.

Beatrice was relieved that at least the house was in order. Mostly. She put away a few things and cleared up clutter, all the while chiding herself that if Edith were upset, the last thing she would be worried about was a coffee mug sitting in the sink and newspapers scattered on the floor. But there was a part of her that hadn't fully made the segue to minster's wife—and a visit was a visit to her, complete with a tidy house.

Edith was right on time with a timid knock at the door, such a light sound that Noo-noo didn't even explode into barking as she usually did. Beatrice opened the door right away and welcomed Edith in as warmly as she could. She recognized Edith as a regular member at the church, but hadn't spoken often to her. Edith had a fluffy halo of white hair and a pleasant, simple face that was now crinkled with grief.

"Edith, it's good to see you," said Wyatt in a warm voice.

"Come on in and sit down," said Beatrice kindly, ushering Edith toward the cushy comfort of the sofa. "Can I get you something to eat or drink?"

Edith shook her head, blinking hard to keep tears at bay.

Edith's color worried Beatrice a bit. She had the feeling that Edith simply didn't want to trouble her. "Tell you what, I'm just going to put some light snacks out and some waters for all of us. I know you might not be feeling hungry, but we have to take care of ourselves, even on the bad days."

Edith gave a hesitant bob of her head and blinked again. Beatrice hurried to her bedroom to grab the tissue box and put it unobtrusively near Edith. Then she walked in the kitchen to try to come up with snacks that might be somewhat healthy and also easy to eat while Wyatt gently started speaking with Edith.

When Beatrice returned with a tray of snack crackers, pretzels, nuts, and waters, Wyatt was in the process of listening and nodding while Edith appeared to be spilling out all sorts of random things about Felton. Edith appeared to be so absorbed in the telling of her story that Beatrice thought she'd not even registered her return—until Edith absently reached out and took some of the pretzels.

"It's just so awful," said Edith, taking one of the tissues and swabbing her eyes. "She was my *friend*. We spent so much time together. I don't feel like a good friend at all now. I should have been there with her."

Shades of Haskell, thought Beatrice. He thought he should have been there to protect her and Edith seemed to think she should have been there to provide emotional support.

Wyatt said, "There was nothing you could have done, Edith. And Felton wouldn't have wanted you to be there to witness that. She was your friend—she wouldn't have wanted to upset you like that."

Edith nodded again and then burst into tears, grabbing the tissue box and pulling it into her lap. Beatrice sat beside her on the sofa and gave her arm a squeeze, looking helplessly at Wyatt.

Crying herself out seemed to work the best, though, and Edith came to a hiccupping stop a few minutes later.

She gingerly blew her nose and looked at both Beatrice and Wyatt apologetically. "I'm so sorry. This was the last thing you needed at the end of the day."

Wyatt said, "This is what I'm here for. I'm so sorry you've lost your friend. Felton was a great woman. We were by there this afternoon with the grandbaby and she invited us into her beautiful yard to see the goldfinches. It was a very kind thing to do."

Edith bobbed her head emphatically. "That's exactly the sort of thing she'd always do. She was so sweet. And really down-to-earth, too, despite everything."

Beatrice asked, "You mean despite her upbringing?"

Edith looked at the floor for a second as if trying to find words there. "Yes. Because of the whole European royalty thing and the money she had. The jewels and things like that. She was always doing nice things for other people. And I know you said I shouldn't feel bad about any of it, but when I think that I was at home heating up a microwave meal when Felton was fighting for her life, I just don't feel like a good friend at all."

Wyatt said quietly, "Sometimes it helps just to talk it out. Would you like to do that? Talk about Felton?"

"Okay." Edith sniffled and then blew her nose again before continuing. "You might not know, but I live right on the other side of Felton. Not the church side, of course, but the other one. So we started out as neighbors."

"And Felton was a good neighbor?" asked Beatrice.

Edith gave a short laugh. "Not really, no. Oh, I feel awful saying that. But the truth is, who would want to live on the other side of that beautiful yard? It made everyone else's yard look terrible in comparison." She quickly added, "Except for the church, of course. The church always looks nice."

"But the church has a yard service and a team of volunteers who come by to tend to it," said Wyatt gently. "You were one person trying to keep up with the yard all by yourself."

Edith gave him a grateful look. "That's right. That makes me feel better, thanks. Anyway, Felton would always speak to me when she saw me out getting my mail or whatever. And we became very good friends." She gave a rather rambling talk for the next ten minutes about the movies she and Felton would see, the times they walked to church together, and their mutual appreciation for quilting.

Beatrice was glad Edith had calmed down, but was starting to feel dangerously close to nodding off, despite the long nap in the hammock earlier. The crazy day had clearly taken something of a toll on her.

When she started paying attention again, Edith added, "And nobody really has any information about what happened. When I talked to Ramsay, he was saying she'd been murdered."

Beatrice and Wyatt stared at her for a few moments. Wyatt said, "He said that?"

"Definitively?" asked Beatrice.

Edith's eyes grew wide at Beatrice's tone and she nodded uncertainly. "Should I not have said anything?"

"No, it's fine, it's just that when we spoke with him, he wasn't positive that was the case," said Beatrice slowly.

Edith's eyes filled with tears again. "It makes it so much worse, doesn't it? It's not just that she had an awful accident or died some sort of natural death. Someone was so upset with her that they *did that*. And I keep thinking about all the good times we had together. She could make some amazing jellies, did you know that? And she canned things. And her stories. Her stories were *wonderful*."

Beatrice nodded, although she felt that Felton's stories were the least-appealing part of Felton.

"Do you have any idea who might have done this?" asked Beatrice quietly. She gave Wyatt an apologetic sideways look since she was causing a major diversion from the ministerial part of the visit.

Edith's face fell and even her fluffy halo of hair seemed to droop. "I just don't know, Beatrice. It's so hard to even think about. Whoever did it must be really, really evil, don't you think, Wyatt?" She looked earnestly at him, waiting for him to weigh in.

Wyatt considered her for a moment before saying, "We don't know exactly what happened. Maybe the person who's responsible didn't mean for this to happen. Maybe it was something that just got out of hand."

"But evil, still, right?" persisted Edith.

"The act of killing is evil," said Wyatt. "I'm not positive it means the person who perpetrates it is. They're still a child of God."

Edith looked at him blankly, seemingly trying to absorb this. She said, "I guess I see what you mean. But I'm not sure if I think it's true. I just don't understand how this could have happened when Felton was alive and well just yesterday." She was silent for a moment and then said, "I'm not trying to say that Felton was a saint. She was a real person and real people have faults. Sometimes she even told tall tales." She gave Wyatt a shy look as if she wasn't sure how he'd react.

He smiled at her and Beatrice said, "I rather wondered about some of the things she said. Of course, I haven't been in Dappled Hills long enough to really know that much about Felton."

Edith said sadly, "It wasn't really her fault—the tall tales. She spoke as she *wanted* things to be, not necessarily how things actually *were*. It all seemed magical to me." Her face was wistful.

"You don't think these tall tales could have somehow gotten her into trouble, do you?" asked Beatrice.

Edith squinted at her, not understanding.

Beatrice continued, "I mean, do you think this might have been a robbery gone wrong? The stories I heard from Felton were usually about her jewelry. Maybe someone decided to try to find the tiara and the ring and the other things and Felton just got in the way."

Edith looked sad. "Maybe. She did talk a lot about her jewelry and people do need money." She hesitated. "I know the yard guy was upset about Felton not paying him. Maybe he went looking for money in the house? I don't know. There was one other thing, too." She stopped and looked worried. "I don't know. I don't think Felton would have wanted me to say anything about it."

"About what?" asked Beatrice.

Edith looked at Wyatt. He said quietly, "She won't know if you mention it now."

Edith took a deep breath. "Well, I went over to visit Felton one day. Not too long ago. The thing about Felton is that she always kept her door unlocked. She even kept it *open* a lot of the time and just had the screen door on to keep bugs out. Anyway, I popped by there without telling her I was going to go. But I did that all the time. She didn't think a thing of it."

Beatrice felt a twinge of impatience. Edith wasn't the best at getting to the heart of a story and the hour was growing later.

Edith frowned. "I don't remember where I was going with this."

Beatrice stifled a sigh and Wyatt said kindly, "You were telling us about going over to see Felton and seeing or hearing something you didn't think Felton would want you to share."

"Oh, right. Thanks. So I went inside and was about to call to Felton to let her know I was there. But I could tell someone was there in the house with Felton so I just sort of stopped cold. I didn't want to intrude, you see. I could hear Felton laughing and I walked toward the sound to see if I should stay or if I should just plan on coming back later. Then I heard this woman's voice and she was positively *ranting* at Felton."

"Ranting at her?" asked Beatrice. "Could you make out what she was saying? Or who she was?"

Edith shook her head slowly. "I couldn't really make out exactly what she was saying. My hearing isn't as good as it used to be. I'm supposed to have an appointment soon to get a pair of hearing aids." She frowned. "I'm not sure when that appointment is, actually. Gosh. Maybe I should call them and get it on my wall calendar."

"But you knew who it was?" asked Beatrice, trying to scrape up the last little bit of her patience.

Edith stared at her blankly. Then she said, "Oh, you mean with Felton. Sorry. Yes, I got just a little bit closer so I could see into the kitchen. It was Rowesa Fant. She works for a friend of Felton's." She looked at the wall clock across from her and then squinted and stared harder at it. "For heaven's sake. Here I am taking up all of your quiet evening time. I'm so very sorry. I really need to go ahead and take my leave."

She stood up and so did Wyatt and Beatrice. Wyatt said, "Are you all right? Feeling any better, Edith?"

Her eyes filled with tears again and she blinked them away. "I'm okay. You were both so kind to let me come over like this. I just wasn't sure what to do. I thought I might feel better if I talked about Felton a little bit. Can we . . . can we say a prayer for her?"

Wyatt led them in a prayer and a few minutes later a grateful Edith took her leave.

Chapter Six

B eatrice walked back over to the sofa and sank down. "Oof. Poor Edith."

"It must be really hard to lose a friend, especially one as close as they were," said Wyatt.

"They seem so very different from each other. I mean, in every way. Felton was always sort of no-nonsense and organized and tough. And then Edith is all fluffy and spacy," said Beatrice.

Wyatt said, "Maybe that's why they got along so well. Because they *weren't* like each other." He paused. "You know, we should probably go by and see Rupert."

"Rupert?" Beatrice frowned.

"Yes. He's Felton's son."

Beatrice blinked at him. "I don't think I even realized Felton *had* a son. I don't recall her ever mentioning him."

Wyatt said slowly, "I'm not sure what their relationship was like. It might simply be that Felton was a very private person when it came to family."

Beatrice snorted. "I doubt that's the case. Not with all her talk of her father's European royalty bloodline. What do you know of her son?"

"Only that he returned to Dappled Hills about a year ago. I understand that he had a successful chain of restaurants, invested too much into expansion, and then went bankrupt. It sounded like one of those cases where he just expanded too quickly for the market."

Beatrice winced. "That's rough. And somehow, I can't think Felton would be the sort of person to let something like that pass. I bet she gave him a hard time about it. For someone like her, appearances would be very important."

Wyatt nodded. "You may be right. But I should still go by there tomorrow. I have the feeling he's going to want to touch base about the funeral service. What are your plans?"

"I have a guild meeting tomorrow, but that's the only thing on the calendar right now. Would you like to go over there with some food tomorrow morning?"

Wyatt said, "I'll call him to make sure, but I think that would work best for my schedule. But don't worry about cooking anything—we can pick something up."

"Do you think a fried chicken meal with all the fixings would work?" asked Beatrice.

"I'm sure it would, or that he'd at least appreciate the gesture."

"It's a plan," said Beatrice.

Wyatt called Rupert the next morning and he asked if they could drop by around ten. It was a Saturday morning, but Wyatt was unusually restless and couldn't sleep in. Beatrice suggested they take Noo-noo on a walk and the crisp morning air, the changing leaves, and the mild exercise seemed to calm Wyatt down.

"Sorry I've been so agitated this morning," he said ruefully.

Beatrice smiled at him. "It's as if you and I have changed places. You're ordinarily the one who's calm in the face of everything and I'm the one who can't sit still."

"And now I have more sympathy for you." Wyatt chuckled.

Beatrice said, "It was just a very unsettled day yesterday and all those folks are members of the church. It means you're having to be more involved in it all."

"After we speak with Rupert this morning, I'll be happy to bow out of it more." He reached out and gave Beatrice's hand a squeeze. He appeared to be eager to change the subject. "Tell me about your guild meeting today."

Beatrice said, "They're probably going to treat me like a long-lost member. I haven't been there for the last couple of months, you know. I think Savannah was about ready to organize a search party."

"I don't remember why it's been so long since you've made a meeting."

Beatrice sighed. "Probably mostly my own lack of inspiration and a slight feeling of guilt that I haven't been working on anything. You know it helps me relax, but I might have burned out a little with all the projects I made before Will was born. Then, after he was born, I was just excited to spend time with him. Then I got that awful cold and didn't go to one of the meetings."

"Anyway," said Wyatt gently, "I know they'll be so glad to see you today. No one is going to give you a hard time about having been away. Everyone's life gets busy sometimes."

"I know. And they're my friends, so they'll just be happy for the chance to catch up. And I will, too. Like I mentioned earlier, I was thinking about the guild meeting the wrong way around. One of the reasons I wasn't going was because I wasn't working on a quilt. But I was forgetting that half the reason a guild meeting is good to go to is because it inspires you to create because you're seeing what everyone *else* is working on."

They walked back down their driveway and Wyatt fished out his key. "Where is the meeting today? Posy's shop?"

"Georgia sent out emails to everyone last night saying she'd have us all over at her house. Posy *was* going to host us at the Patchwork Cottage, but I think Georgia was being thoughtful after Posy's rough day yesterday. She said it was because she and Tony had done some redecorating and she wanted us to see it, but I think it's because she didn't want Posy to have to worry about setting up for the meeting."

"That sounds like something Georgia would do," said Wyatt. He looked at his watch. "Should we head out and pick up the fried chicken order on the way over to see Rupert?"

They got Noo-noo settled in the house and headed out.

After picking up the meal, Wyatt drove to a small house on a street that backed up to theirs and Felton's. The brick home looked as if it had seen better days with landscaping that wasn't being kept up and ivy running rampant over the house. The back of the property edged up to the back of Felton's.

Wyatt said, "This is actually a piece of property that Felton owned. She told me one day that she let Rupert stay here when he returned to town after his restaurants had failed."

Beatrice surveyed the house and grounds. "I can't even associate this house with Felton in any way. Her house is so beautifully-maintained and she took such good care of it."

Wyatt nodded. "She told me that she'd had a tenant who hadn't been good about tending to the house. She gave him a couple of weeks' notice to move out once she found out her son was coming back to Dappled Hills."

They walked up the narrow walkway to the house and Wyatt knocked. A dark-haired, slim, middle-aged man with a mustache and a mouth that drew down at the corners answered the door. He was neatly attired in khaki pants and a blue button-down shirt, almost as if it were a familiar uniform that he hadn't gotten out of the habit of wearing.

He reached out a hand and shook Wyatt's and took the food out of Beatrice's hands. "Thanks so much to you both for coming by. Please come inside."

The inside of the house was dim and it took a moment for Beatrice's eyes to adjust. When they did, she saw an almost-bare living room with a single chair. From what she could see of the kitchen, it looked equally bare.

Rupert came back from putting the food away and said in an embarrassed tone, "I'm so sorry about the seating situation."

"It's no problem at all," said Wyatt quickly. "It will do us good to stand for a while."

Beatrice added, "Yes, I've been thinking recently how much sitting I do. I never used to have such a sedentary life. We have a new grandbaby and the stroller rides and walks with the dog seem to be the only times I'm even getting any exercise."

"I was thinking about getting a standing desk," said Wyatt.

Rupert's solemn features broke into a grin, "All right, all right, you've convinced me. Thanks for being so understanding." He hesitated. "I'm guessing you're here about the service for Mother?"

Wyatt said, "That too, but mainly Beatrice and I wanted to convey our sympathy for you and to see if there was anything we could do. There are committees at the church for bringing food to grieving families and I'll be in contact with them, of course. There's also a ministry that serves as an ear for members and families going through hard times, if you're interested in that."

"I've certainly been through a hard time, although I'm not sure if my particular hard time is exactly what the ministry is looking for," said Rupert ruefully.

Wyatt said, "It's for *any* type of rough patch people go through. And my door is always open, too."

Rupert nodded. "I do really appreciate this. It hasn't been an easy year—any of it. And frankly, the most overwhelming feeling I'm experiencing right now with Mother's death is guilt."

Beatrice remembered Edith sharing the same feeling.

Wyatt said, "That's very common. From my time in the church, I've heard many members of the congregation expressing the same thing."

Rupert said, "It's just that Mother and I weren't on the best of terms and now she's gone. And gone in such a violent manner—the police told me she'd been murdered. I was here at the house, right in her backyard, but didn't help her."

Wyatt said, "She wouldn't have wanted you to be put into any danger, Rupert."

Rupert gave a short laugh. "Wouldn't she? I don't know, sometimes I think she felt she'd be better off without me."

"You were her only child, weren't you?" asked Beatrice softly. "I'm sure she didn't feel that way."

Rupert sighed. "We had a very complicated relationship. You may have heard about my business troubles. Mother spread them all over town."

Wyatt and Beatrice didn't say anything and Rupert continued, "I expanded my restaurants too quickly and ended up not being able to support them. I declared bankruptcy and had to come home with my tail between my legs."

Wyatt said, "That must have been very hard."

"It was. I hate asking anyone for help, especially my mother. And here I was, a grown man, having to move back to the town he'd left when he was a teenager. I never really came home again after I went off to college, except for holidays and Mother's odd birthday or so. I don't know a soul here now. I was angry and bitter about it and she didn't help matters at all."

"What happened?" asked Beatrice.

"Oh, I tried to get her to tell a cover story about why I'd come back home. That I was here to take care of her or to be close with her. But she'd hear nothing of it. She told everyone that I'd failed at business and was back home because I was totally broke. If I'd even *wanted* to make friends with people in town before, I certainly didn't feel I could do it then. I was too humiliated," said Rupert.

Beatrice said, "At least it's good that you have your own place here. I'd think that would provide more of a feeling of independence."

"I'd rather have been in the main house where there is actual furniture and cookware and things like that. I even asked Mother if I could go through her attic to see if there was anything up there that wasn't being used that I could bring over here, but she wouldn't hear a thing of it. She acted suspicious, as if I was going to go upstairs and rob her of all her 'precious jewels.'" The end of his sentence was said in a bitter tone.

"Wasn't there some nice jewelry in the house, though? I know Felton mentioned she had some really lovely pieces," said Beatrice.

"I've no doubt she did," said Rupert. "But the fact of the matter is that even if she *did* have some nice jewelry, she clearly sold it off at some point. I didn't see it."

"But you probably saw it when you were growing up, right?" asked Beatrice.

He shook his head. "I don't remember it. Maybe she had it and didn't show me. Maybe she realized that I really didn't care all that much about the stuff. Or, frankly, about the family history she was always trying to shove down my throat. Another thing—you'll probably think this is extremely early, but I spoke to Mother's lawyer yesterday after I spoke with the funeral home. That must seem awful, but you don't know the financial straits I've been in."

Judging from the house and its lack of contents, Beatrice suspected it must have been pretty bad.

He sighed. "Anyway, if Mother did have money, it's just like the jewelry; it's gone now. She didn't have anything. In fact, I might have to borrow money just to pay for her funeral costs. I had no idea she was in a situation like that. And she thought *I'd* been irresponsible."

Beatrice said, "But surely the house—if you sold the house and its contents, everything should work out."

Rupert shook his head. "She had mortgaged the house to the hilt and the credit card bills I saw in the house really scared me yesterday. It's a real mess."

He paused and then gave a short laugh. "I'm sorry. You can see why I'm feeling guilty. I just can't seem to stop myself from being bitter, no matter what time period in my life I'm remembering. And Mother's dead. You'd think I could put it all behind me."

"I think that's easier said than done," said Wyatt, giving him a smile. "And it sounds as if you've had plenty to be upset about. Maybe with time you can feel a little differently about it all."

"I hope so," said Rupert in a doubtful voice. He said, "As far as the service goes, Mother wanted to be cremated and have her ashes spread over the garden. So I suppose a memorial service would be in order." He pushed a hand through his dark hair. "Not that I have any idea whatsoever how to do that."

Wyatt said, "The funeral home will take care of all the details once you make arrangements with them. And I'd be happy to conduct the service, if you'd like. We can keep it very simple if you don't have any specific requests or know of anything your mother would like to have included."

Rupert shook his head. "She never talked about her service, as far as I'm aware. If you could take care of it, that would be wonderful." He shook his head. "I just want all this to be over and I know that's not a good attitude."

"I think it's a very natural one," said Wyatt.

Rupert sighed. "The whole thing has been such a nightmare and now there's going to be an investigation, which means there won't be any real closure anytime soon—not even with the memorial service. I hope they figure out who did this as fast as they can."

Beatrice said, "Did your mother mention anything that might give a clue as to who's behind this?"

An unguarded look that Beatrice couldn't decipher crossed his features before it disappeared. Rupert snorted. "That's the thing. We weren't really communicating. The only person I know she spent a good deal of time with was Edith, but she's her best friend."

"Has she ever mentioned a Rowesa?" asked Beatrice, trying to sound casual.

Rupert's face went blank. "Rowesa? No. I'm sorry, but as I said before, I haven't been in this town for longer than a couple of days for decades. I don't really know anyone here."

Wyatt said kindly, "You know we'd be glad to have you come to the church if you're wanting to meet people. If you're not interested in services, there are plenty of other activities you could be involved in. We have exercise classes and jogging clubs and other things we host."

Rupert gave him a smile. "I'll think about it. Thanks."

Chapter Seven

A few minutes later, Wyatt and Beatrice walked back to the car.

"I'm not sure what to make of all that," said Beatrice as Wyatt drove away.

"In what way?" asked Wyatt.

"I don't know. I mean, I totally understand his not having a great relationship with his mother. I found Felton difficult to get along with, too. But I'm pretty stunned she was in such bad financial trouble. She always painted a totally different picture of herself. Maybe she wasn't happy about Rupert coming back to town because she was worried he'd be even more of a drain on her limited resources," said Beatrice.

Wyatt said, "It may have happened over a period of some years. Maybe she wasn't left in good financial shape when her parents passed away."

Beatrice frowned. "Had she ever held a job?"

Wyatt considered this and then shook his head. "Not as far as I'm aware. I figured she was just living off of her inheritance."

"Which must have dried up long ago. And she may not have helped things with her spending habits. That car of hers is very expensive for someone who rarely drove."

Wyatt said, "It must have been quite a blow for Rupert. He must have been thinking that at least he should be able to be in a better situation, if nothing else. But now it sounds as if he's even deeper in a hole."

After Wyatt dropped Beatrice off at the house, he headed off to the church while she freshened up to go to the guild meeting at Georgia's house. She took Noo-noo for a brief walk and then hopped in the car and headed off.

Georgia's house was a cute gray house with white trim. Beatrice remembered that the house had been a fixer-upper, but Georgia had certainly married the right man to help with that. Tony had worked at the hardware store for years and seemed to know everything about home improvement. Georgia had said the yard had also been a disaster, but it had been neatly cleared out and lots of young plants were growing.

Georgia greeted her cheerily at the door, her pretty face lighting up in pleasure at showing the work she'd put into the new house.

"I'm so glad you're hosting today because I've been dying to see your new place," said Beatrice.

Georgia beamed at her. "And I've been dying to show it off! Come on in."

Beatrice's first impression was that it was about 180 degrees different from poor Rupert's place. Instead of dim lighting, there was lots of natural light coming through the large windows. Semi-sheer shades were pulled up to allow the sunshine in. The walls were painted a warm beige and the sofa was a cheerful light-blue checkered pattern. The quilts Georgia had chosen to display lent the whole room a cozy feel. As Georgia showed Beatrice the rest of the house, the cheeriness and warmth was reflected in every room.

"I love it," said Beatrice, giving her a hug. "And I especially love that it looks like *you*."

Georgia said, "I'm so glad to hear you say that! If you'd known how much time Tony and I put into it. I don't think I really realized what I was taking on before I started it."

Beatrice said ruefully, "I can only imagine. I know how much suffering Wyatt and I endured over a simple kitchen remodel and we didn't even do the work ourselves."

Georgia said, "That's the nice thing about having Tony be so handy. I don't have to wait for the contractor to show up because he's already here! Of course, there were some things he wasn't qualified to do, but he did almost everything."

The doorbell rang and the next few minutes were filled with guild members coming in. Georgia had set up a table with snacks and drinks and everyone gravitated in that direction.

There was a woman there wearing black slacks, a white blouse, and a pretty, colorful scarf. She had a bright smile and twinkling eyes. Beatrice didn't know her, but everyone else seemed to.

Georgia said, "Beatrice, let me introduce you to Chrissy Jo."

Chrissy Jo shook hands with her and Georgia added, "She grew up here in Dappled Hills but moved away after she got married."

Chrissy Jo smiled at her. "But I'm back here as much as I can."

Georgia added, "Beatrice is from Atlanta and retired here to be near her daughter. And now, her cute grandbaby." She excused herself to greet other members as they came in.

"Are you a quilter?" asked Beatrice.

Chrissy Jo said, "I love to quilt. It helps me relax when life gets really crazy."

Beatrice nodded. "Me too. Which is something I need to remember because life is crazy right now and I haven't been quilting at all."

"Are you feeling more stressed than you would if you'd been quilting?"

"Definitely," said Beatrice wryly. "A clear sign I need to get back into it." She smiled at Chrissy Jo. "What brings you back to town? Just trying to catch up with everyone?"

Chrissy Jo said, "That, too. I love seeing everybody. But my aunt passed away a few months ago. I'm here to help go through her things."

"Sorry to hear that. I didn't know."

Chrissy Jo said, "There's no reason you would. Anyway, that's what brought me here this time. I think it's going to take a while to go through everything. My aunt was something of a collector."

Georgia returned to their conversation and raised her eyebrows at the word *collector*. "You're in the right spot, then! Beatrice was an art museum curator."

Chrissy Jo chuckled. "I'm not sure any of my aunt's things qualify as art, unfortunately. She collected things that were in-

teresting to her, but might not be as interesting to anybody else."
She hesitated. "But there might be one or two things I wouldn't
mind passing by you."

Beatrice said, "Sure. I could run by the house at some point."

Chrissy Jo shook her head. "Thanks for offering, but I'd hate
to inconvenience you. Would it be okay if I texted you pictures
and you could see what you think?"

They exchanged phone numbers and then Posy walked over
to give Chrissy Jo a hug.

Beatrice chatted for a while with Savannah, Georgia's sister.
Despite being sisters, they were about as different from each
other as it was possible to be. Georgia was sweet and patient,
and made an excellent elementary school teacher. Savannah was
exacting and hard-featured. She had a kind heart, but could
seem brusque when you didn't know her. Beatrice paused and
glanced up when she heard Piper's voice.

Savannah gave a delighted gasp. "She has the baby with
her!"

Suddenly, there was rapid movement from the entire guild
away from the refreshments table and toward Piper and baby
Will.

"I didn't just bring Will," said Piper with a grin as Ash came
in the door behind her, loaded down with a quilt and various
baby paraphernalia.

Meadow came in right behind Ash. "I told them to bring
the baby and if he fusses, I'll take him on a walk," said Meadow
grinning.

Beatrice had the feeling that Meadow would be absolutely
delighted if Will were to start fussing. Her brow wrinkled as she

noticed that Meadow had had time to not only finish one quilt but start another. And Meadow had been babysitting Will even more than Beatrice had.

Georgia gave everyone a quick tour of her house and everyone oohed and ahhed when they weren't cooing over the baby. Beatrice stayed in the front of the house and helped herself to a plate of delicious looking snacks. Georgia had really gone all out, despite the short notice and had put out all sorts of goodies.

Ash put down all the baby things and grabbed a plate, too. He gave Beatrice a quick hug. "How are you doing? Piper filled me in about yesterday."

"Oh, I'm fine, although it was a crazy day. Poor Felton." She looked closer at Ash. "How are you and Piper looking so fresh and awake? I thought all parents of babies looked sleep-deprived and frazzled."

"Well, catch me around suppertime and I'll probably look frazzled." He chuckled. "Will usually rants a little bit around 5p.m. Our pediatrician calls it 'happy hour.' But he sleeps really well at night. I'm more of a night owl and Piper is a morning lark and so I give him a late feeding before I turn in and he's fine until Piper gets up with him early in the morning."

Beatrice was impressed. "I guess it just goes to show that—"

"He's the best baby ever," chimed in Meadow, walking up to them holding Will, her eyes twinkling. "Don't I keep saying that? I don't even want to think about all the nights I was wandering through the house, holding Ash and trying to get him to fall asleep. He seemed fiercely opposed to sleep of any kind, simply as a matter of principle."

Ash gazed proudly at Will. "He's just a really easy little guy. He's happy most of the time. Sleeps well at night, takes naps, likes trying baby foods."

"Perfect," summed up Meadow.

Beatrice glanced over at the mountain of baby equipment that Ash had brought in. "Is that a quilt over there?" She frowned.

Ash nodded his head, looking proud again. "That's right. Piper and I thought we'd try to keep up the co-quilting that we were doing. It's kind of fun to make something together and goes a lot faster than it would with just one of us working on it. And Posy stocked up all kinds of masculine-looking fabrics to help me out." He chuckled and Will gurgled in response.

"I'd love to see what you're working on," said Beatrice. "I've gotten in sort of a rut and I need some inspiration to get out of it." She chuckled. "Actually, I'm also getting inspiration from the fact that you and Piper are working on a quilt despite having a baby in the house."

Ash turned to get the quilt out and Miss Sissy walked up to Meadow who was jiggling Will and talking softly to him. Miss Sissy was a very old woman of indeterminate age. And very stubborn.

Miss Sissy glared at Meadow. "I want to hold the baby."

Meadow gave Miss Sissy a doubtful look. Miss Sissy didn't exactly look like the posterchild of the world's best babysitter. In fact, today she looked rather dangerous with her stormy expression. She was wearing a long black dress that she'd apparently spilled her breakfast on and her hair was coming out in wiry strands from the bun she'd made so that most of her hair was on her shoulders instead of in the bun at all.

"Maybe in a little while," said Meadow. "Don't you want to get a plate of food? It's all really good."

If there was one thing healthy about Miss Sissy, it was her appetite. She could eat anyone under the table. Where the calories ended up, however, was a mystery. Miss Sissy's frame was stick-thin.

"Already ate," said Miss Sissy. "Two times."

"Well, how about if I let you hold Will after the meeting?" Will was starting to fuss a little and Meadow swung him around and gave him another jiggle.

Miss Sissy's eyes narrowed. "Want to hold him now."

"Oh for heaven's sake, Meadow," said Beatrice. "Let's find Miss Sissy a comfortable spot to sit down and let her hold the baby."

Meadow reluctantly followed Beatrice and Miss Sissy over to the blue and white sofa while Will made little protesting fussy noises. Miss Sissy plopped down and Beatrice carefully put pillows under both of the old woman's skinny elbows. "There."

Meadow gingerly handed Will over to Miss Sissy. Will put his thumb in his mouth and looked up curiously at the old woman as she beamed at him.

"Now, he's sometimes a little spitty, so let's get you a cloth," said Meadow.

Miss Sissy scowled at her. "Don't need one."

"If he gets fussy, I'll come by and take him from you. It's getting close to his naptime," said Meadow.

Miss Sissy didn't deign to answer her, but continued smiling down at the baby.

Beatrice walked back over to where Ash and Piper were standing with the quilt as Meadow hovered anxiously by Miss Sissy.

"Would you look at that," said Ash with a chuckle, looking over at Miss Sissy and Will.

Piper pulled out her phone. "I have to take a picture."

Ash said, "She's like the baby whisperer. Will got quiet right away."

Beatrice said wryly, "He's probably wondering who on earth is holding him."

Miss Sissy did have a very interesting face, deeply crevassed with lines that seemed to tell a story. Will was mesmerized.

"So, the quilt," said Beatrice.

Ash and Piper held it out between them.

"You did a great job with it," said Beatrice warmly. "I love the pattern . . . that's a True North Compass block, isn't it?"

"You've got it," said Ash with a grin.

The colors were warm and rich with chocolatey brown paisley prints and blacks offset by the creamy white of the compass star block.

Posy walked up to them and Beatrice was glad to see her friend looked back to normal today, except for looking a little tired, as if she might not have had a full night's sleep.

"It's beautiful," said Posy. "And I just love that the two of you worked on it together. What a wonderful project for a couple!"

Ash said, "Quilting is actually really relaxing for me. I didn't think it would be—I thought it would be just one more thing on my list that I needed to do. But I love that we're creating something, together."

Piper looked over at the baby and her eyes opened wide. "Can you believe it?"

They turned to see Will, totally asleep and sucking on his thumb as Miss Sissy gazed tenderly down at him.

"I'm taking another picture," said Piper, pushing buttons on her phone.

"Like I said, she's the baby whisperer," said Ash with an admiring shake of his head.

Savannah came up to Miss Sissy and she glowered and hissed at her so Savannah jumped back, nearly running into her friend and fellow quilter Edgenora, who was also hoping to see the baby.

"I can see how this is going to go," said Beatrice wryly. "Miss Sissy is going to be the gatekeeper and guard Will from everyone at the meeting."

"Well, he could use a good nap," said Piper. "I guess that's one way for him to get one."

Beatrice said, "He's so soundly asleep, even though it's incredibly noisy in here. What a gift!"

Savannah and Edgenora gave up trying to see the baby and came over to speak with Piper and Ash, instead. Posy pulled Beatrice aside.

"I don't want to bring up what happened yesterday in front of everyone—it would be a sad thing to talk about on a fun occasion like this. But I just wanted to let you know how grateful I am to you yesterday for helping me out," said Posy earnestly.

Beatrice said, "But that's what friends are for. I was happy to help. It made me feel helpless, and helping you at least made me feel as if I were doing *something*. I'm glad you're better today."

Posy said sadly, "Not well enough to handle the guild meeting, though. Poor Georgia. I really appreciate her, too."

"I think she was delighted to host. She's probably been hoping for a good chance to show everyone what she and Tony have done with the house and this was exactly the opportunity she needed to actually follow through with it."

Posy gave her a smile. "How are things going with you? Did you bring anything here for the show and tell?"

The show and tell part of the program was when the quilters shared what they'd finished and what they were currently working on. This was actually one of the parts Beatrice was most looking forward to, since she was hoping to get a little inspiration from everyone else's projects.

"I didn't," said Beatrice with a grimace. "All the projects I'd been working on I gave to Piper and Ash for Will, so I don't have anything to show for myself. And, like I said, I've been in a sort of rut lately, so I'm not working on anything now."

Posy considered this, thoughtfully. "Do you think it might help if you could work on something really easy, just to get unblocked? Something that could be started and finished in very little time?"

"Honestly, that's probably *exactly* what I need. The prep work is definitely part of my block—I don't want to think about figuring out the fabric or the size or the design. It's all making me feel overwhelmed. What do you suggest for something quick and easy?"

Posy said tentatively, "How about a strip quilt? You probably have a lot of leftover baby-print fabric from the projects you did before Will was born. What if you pieced them together to make a small quilt?"

Meadow popped up to join them and overheard what Posy had said. "Oooh, that's a terrific idea, Beatrice."

"But Piper and Ash have lots of little quilts for Will," said Beatrice. "I like the idea of making something useful."

"No, it *would* be useful," said Meadow. "When Piper came to pick up Will yesterday, she was telling me how spitty he is around meals. She's had the quilts constantly in the wash and she likes to have him sit on a quilt when he's having floor time. It sounded like it would help for them to have more so she wouldn't have to do laundry all the time."

Posy added, "And the prints don't even have to match with a strip quilt. You just pin and sew and press the seams. Make them into blocks, then sew the blocks together."

"So, machine-quilt it?" asked Beatrice.

"Oh, I think definitely, don't you? You need a quick project and I do believe that's the way to go," said Posy.

"Thanks," said Beatrice with a smile. "I knew I'd get ideas if I came to the meeting."

"Yes, and don't skip any more guild meetings!" said Meadow sternly. "That doesn't help things. And now I'm going over to love on my darling grandbaby."

"Meadow, I wouldn't do that," said Beatrice quickly, but Meadow was already setting out with great determination toward Will.

Sure enough, as soon as she got within a couple of feet of the baby, Miss Sissy hissed violently at her, startling Meadow away.

"Maybe I need to keep Miss Sissy at my house when I'm babysitting Will," said Beatrice with a chuckle to Georgia. "She'd keep Meadow at bay."

"And anyone else who wanted to see Will," said Georgia wryly. She glanced at her watch and cleared her throat. "I think we'd better go ahead and get started, everybody. Some of our group is already falling asleep from waiting."

There was a wave of laughter from the group as everyone looked over at Will. Miss Sissy eyed them all with hostility as if they might come over and try to give the baby a cuddle.

Chapter Eight

They all took seats and the meeting began. Meadow gave details about an upcoming service project the guild was undertaking and Savannah gave information (in a staccato, bullet-point fashion) on the quilt show they'd all be participating in after a few months.

During the show-and-tell portion of the meeting, everyone took turns showing their quilts and talking about what they were working on. Georgia held up a quilted wall hanging in a sea blue with a cute pattern of fish, crabs, and sea horses. "I thought this would be fun to hang up. Tony's favorite place is the beach and I figured this would be a great way to make him feel like he was getting a little taste of it here at home."

Beatrice added the wall hanging to her mental list of quick and easy projects. It was a lot smaller than a quilt and shouldn't take much time. She felt even more motivated after seeing a cute bandana quilt Piper had made in a few hours and a tee shirt memory quilt Meadow put together with a bunch of Ash's old high school and college tee shirts.

When the meeting wrapped up, Edgenora came up to speak with Beatrice. "Is everything going all right? Wyatt told me you were there yesterday with Felton. That must have been awful."

Beatrice nodded. "Not as bad as it was for poor Posy, of course."

"Or Felton," added Edgenora dryly.

"Exactly. Wyatt and I ran by to speak with Felton's son this morning and I believe Wyatt was going to check in to see if we could arrange more food for Rupert. Felton was such a loyal member of the church that I know the members want to do something for her son."

Edgenora said, "Wyatt has already made the calls. He's been very organized today."

"That's good to hear," said Beatrice. She paused. She knew Edgenora knew just about everyone at the church from her role as the secretary. "I have a quick question for you. I'm sure you know Betty Lamar. Do you know her son, Haskell?"

Edgenora made a face and then apologized. "Sorry, that was rude of me. Yes, I do know him, I'm afraid. He's not my favorite member of youth group, I can tell you that."

"What's he done?" asked Beatrice curiously. Whatever it was must have been fairly egregious since Edgenora was usually very circumspect in terms of what she said about members of the congregation.

"I just disapproved of the way he spoke to his mother. You know how much Betty does for the church and I have so much respect for her. But I've heard him speak to Betty in an absolutely horrible way a couple of different times when he thought no one was around in the church office. The tone of his voice and the language he used?" She shook her head and narrowed her eyes.

"That's terrible. And surprising. When Wyatt and I spoke with him recently, butter would melt in his mouth."

Edgenora gave a stern nod. "Exactly. He's two-faced, depending who's around him. The perfect teenager on one hand and the disrespectful son on the other. Again, I hate to speak that way about a young member of our church, but it's the truth."

She seemed eager to change the subject and was soon talking about church business—upcoming events and how various hospitalized members of the congregation were doing until she became absorbed in another conversation with Meadow and Posy.

Beatrice watched as Will lazily woke up, staring in wide-eyed interest at Miss Sissy's grizzled visage beaming down at him. Beatrice cautiously walked over and perched on the sofa next to Miss Sissy, relieved that she wasn't hissed at.

"When are you watching him next?" asked the old woman.

"Will? Oh, I'm keeping him Monday morning," said Beatrice. She stifled a sigh, guessing the reason for Miss Sissy's interest.

"I'll visit." Miss Sissy's voice was firm, brooking no disagreement.

Beatrice helpfully pointed out, "I believe Meadow is keeping him for a couple of hours tomorrow, after church. Piper and Ash had some errands to run."

Miss Sissy shook her head violently, causing even more strands of wiry gray hair to cascade out of the very messy bun. "She isn't fair."

"Isn't *fair*?"

"Won't let me hold him long." Miss Sissy's eyes gleamed with malevolence.

"Well, if you come by day-after-tomorrow, I'll let you hold him as long as you want. And maybe we can take some stroller rides. He's so cute in the stroller and loves being out in nature. Would you be up to a walk?"

Miss Sissy gave her a reproving look as if to say she was in perfect health and completely fit and able to participate in a stroller ride.

Savannah hesitantly approached, giving Miss Sissy a cautious look in case she chased her off again. She smiled at Beatrice. "I heard what you said about Will loving nature. I was wondering if I could come by the house with little Smoke?"

Smoke was Savannah's much-beloved gray cat. Georgia had made all sorts of little bowties and outfits for Smoke and the good-natured cat almost looked like a baby doll.

Miss Sissy growled at this and Savannah gave her a leery look before continuing, "It's just that he's so soft and I thought I could help teach Will how to be gentle with animals. You know how patient Smoke is."

"He's already around animals," muttered the old woman.

Savannah blinked at this.

"He's used to Noo-noo and Boris, Meadow's dog. But I'm not sure he's ever seen a cat up close. I think he'd love that.

Thanks, Savannah," said Beatrice. "I was just telling Miss Sissy that I'd be keeping Will on Monday."

Miss Sissy scowled at having her time with the baby interrupted.

Savannah quickly said, "I won't want to *hold* Will, Miss Sissy. Just to show him the kitty and how to be sweet to Smoke since he loves animals. You can hold him and I'll show him the cat."

Miss Sissy grudgingly acquiesced, looking a bit more cheerful about the upcoming visit.

Soon everyone started leaving Georgia's house and heading back home. On the way out, Chrissy Jo walked up to Beatrice and said softly, "Posy told me what happened yesterday. It just breaks my heart. I saw Felton just a couple of days ago. She seemed so happy, talking about her garden and planning what she'd plant next spring. We talked about our favorite tomato varieties." Chrissy Jo sighed. "Now she'll never get to plant that garden."

"I know," said Beatrice. "When I saw her shortly before she died, she was so sweet to my grandbaby and showing him around her garden. It's all very sad."

Chrissy Jo said, "How is Edith doing? Do you know her? She was very close to Felton. She must be feeling terrible now. I'll have to run by and visit her."

"I'm sure she'd love that. And be sure to send those pictures of the collectibles from your aunt when you have a chance," said Beatrice, surprising herself. Usually it made her uncomfortable when people asked her advice on the value of their things because so frequently it wasn't worth anything. Maybe she missed her work on some level and was looking forward to the chance to briefly appraise something.

When Beatrice pulled into the driveway, she saw Noo-noo in the large picture window at the front of the house, beaming at her, which made Beatrice smile, too. That was the great thing about dogs—they were always so happy to see you.

She was climbing out of her car when another car pulled into the driveway. Beatrice turned with surprise and was even more surprised when she saw the visitor was Rowesa Fant. Rowesa gave her a quick wave and attempted a smile, but it wasn't much of a smile and Beatrice thought she looked pale.

Beatrice waited while Rowesa climbed out of the older model car, bearing a basket of eggs. Rowesa was in her 30s with shoulder-length brown hair that forever seemed to be covering up her face. She gave Beatrice another smile, this one broader. "I was gathering eggs this morning from my chickens and thought I'd run them by for you and Wyatt."

Beatrice carefully took the basket of eggs. "That's so sweet of you. Thank you."

Rowesa hesitated and Beatrice quickly asked, "Can you come in for a few minutes? If you distract our corgi, it will be a huge help—I won't endanger the eggs."

Rowesa, now more relaxed, nodded. "Corgis are so cute. I'd love to visit with him."

And so Beatrice was able to get inside the house without breaking an egg as Noo-noo threw herself on her back so Rowesa could give her a tummy rub.

Beatrice put the eggs in the fridge and then joined Rowesa again. "Why don't we go into the living room and visit? Do you have time?"

Rowesa flushed and said, "Oh, I hate to take up your afternoon."

"I promise I don't have anything important to do. If I don't visit with you, I'm going to start feeling guilty again for not working on a quilt like everyone else in my guild," said Beatrice with a smile. "Can I get you something to eat or drink?"

Rowesa hastily said she was fine and sat gingerly on the sofa as if she were a child at the principal's office. She tentatively asked, "Is Wyatt home? I saw his car outside."

Beatrice said, "He's actually over at the church; he just walked over there this morning. Did you need to speak with him? I could give him a call."

Rowesa's flush deepened. "I don't want to disturb him."

"A minister's life is all about being disturbed. He won't look at it like that at all, anyway—his favorite thing about the job is listening to and helping others. I'll phone him."

Beatrice was just dialing his number when the front door opened and Wyatt was there with a smile, curiously looking in to see who the car in the driveway belonged to.

Rowesa got to her feet as Noo-noo trotted over to greet Wyatt. He gave the little dog a rub and said, "Rowesa, good to see you."

"I was just about to call you," said Beatrice. She stood up and said to Rowesa, "I'll let the two of you visit for a bit."

Rowesa shook her head. "If you don't mind, would you stay, too? You always seem so level-headed. I'd like to hear what you have to say. I mean . . . unless you have some other things you need to be doing, of course."

"I'm delighted to procrastinate doing the laundry," said Beatrice, giving her a warm smile in the hopes the younger woman would finally start to relax.

But it seemed as if relaxing was not in Rowesa's future. She twisted her hands together in her lap and looked anxiously at Wyatt and Beatrice through her hair.

"I don't even know where to begin," she started slowly. "And I'm not looking forward to talking about this. I thought it would make me feel better to talk about it, but now I don't know. I'll hate having you look at me differently. Having *everyone* look at me differently." She bent her head down further and now her hair completely obscured her face. Noo-noo seemed to sense her feelings and lay down on top of her feet. Rowesa bent down to rub him.

Wyatt said gently, "I promise you're in a safe place here. We're not here to judge you. We just want to help."

Beatrice added, "Maybe start at the beginning? We have the time."

Rowesa looked up, giving them both a grateful look. "Thanks." She took a deep breath. "First off, I don't know if you remember since there are a lot of church members, but I'm a single mom. I have a little girl, Ashley." She smiled, just thinking of her.

Beatrice nodded. "I remember. She's absolutely precious. Blonde hair and the cutest little dresses at church."

"I make those myself," said Rowesa a note of pride in her voice. Then she grew solemn again. "The problem is that there's never enough money to go around. I've cut just about every-where I can cut. I don't run the air conditioner or the heater. We eat canned soup most nights that I get when there's a sale. And I work a couple of different jobs. But you know how expensive childcare is. There was a lady who was watching Ashley for me for a while, but then she moved away with her husband and I had to sign Ashley up at a daycare center."

Wyatt said softly, "I'd imagine that's taking up a good deal of your income every week."

Rowesa nodded. "But I needed her to be in a good place, a safe place. I've already run my credit card as high as it can go, paying for it on the weeks when I just didn't have enough money in my bank account—you know, when Ashley and I would have to go to the doctor or something. Now I don't have any credit left and I can barely make the minimum payments on the card. Then my car broke down again and I had to get it repaired so I could get to work."

"When it rains, it pours." Beatrice shook her head.

"And I kept telling myself that things were going to get bet-ter soon because Ashley will be able to go to public kindergarten next fall and I won't have to pay for child care—just after-school care, which is much less-expensive. But that's a whole year away and I felt like I just couldn't make it." She dipped her head down again. "That's when I did it."

Wyatt and Beatrice sat quietly, waiting for Rowesa to ex-plain. It seemed to take her a few moments to gather herself to be able to do so. But finally, she lifted her head and looked at them again.

"One of my odd jobs is to help a senior citizen out with her errands. Her name is Lucy Bradwell; you probably know her?"

Wyatt and Beatrice nodded.

Rowesa took another deep breath. "She doesn't drive anymore and she needed help picking up groceries and her medicines from the pharmacy. Dropping off packages at the post office and things like that."

Beatrice thought that this was exactly the job Haskell had with Felton.

"Mrs. Bradwell has always been so sweet to me," said Rowesa in a somewhat strangled voice. "Really kind. She's even tried to help me out by sending me home with food for Ashley and me. She's given me extra money on Ashley's birthday." A single tear ran down Rowesa's face. "She *trusted* me."

Beatrice had the feeling she knew what Rowesa was going to say next.

"But one day, something came over me. I felt so desperate. It's no excuse, but I was totally exhausted—I'd been up the whole night the night before, worried about how I was going to be able to pay my rent that month. And where Ashley and I could go if I couldn't pay it. Mrs. Bradwell asked me to run an errand to the bank for her—to take her ATM card and get cash out to pay her yardman with." She shook her head, looking angry at herself.

Wyatt and Beatrice nodded in encouragement.

"And I ran the errand like I had twenty times before. Except *this* time, I took out more than she asked me for and I pocketed the rest." A deep red flush of shame covered Rowesa's face and neck and she looked anxiously over at Wyatt and Beatrice.

Wyatt said, "What a terrible burden you've been carrying."

Another tear slid down Rowesa's face. "You're being kind. I stole from Mrs. Bradwell. I took money from someone who'd been nothing but generous to me. I felt so sick over it right after I'd done it that I thought I'd go back, tell her I'd made a mistake, and hand over the whole amount."

"Was that what you ended up doing?" asked Beatrice.

Rowesa gave a short laugh. "Well, it was what I *wanted* to do. But at the ATM, I took some of the money out and put it in my purse. The rest I put in an envelope to hand over to Mrs. Bradwell. It was almost as if I was doing it automatically. Part of me still said I was going to hand over the whole amount to her, but maybe I wanted the feel of money in my pocket for once. I don't know what was going through my head." She paused. "The thing was, someone saw me."

Chapter Nine

Beatrice frowned. "But surely it wasn't obvious what you were doing. You might have been getting money out of the ATM for yourself, after all."

Rowesa shook her head. "It was Felton Billows. She's a friend of Mrs. Bradwell and knows I'm her errand-runner, just like that teen boy is hers. She watched me separate the money out."

Beatrice persisted, "But still, you could have been separating it out for your own purposes. Maybe you had a specific amount you were setting aside to pay for your rent or your childcare."

"The problem is that she immediately called me on it. I didn't realize she was there because I had my back to her, of course, so I didn't have time to come up with a lie or to even tell her it was my own transaction. Mrs. Billows immediately said, 'That's Mrs. Bradwell's money, isn't it? Why are you taking some of it?' I felt myself turn red all over. I was just so ashamed and already felt so guilty that it wasn't possible for me to brush it off or tell her I was running my own errand," said Rowesa.

Wyatt said slowly, "I thought Felton wasn't driving herself anymore."

"Oh, she wasn't by herself. The teen boy was in the car, waiting. He was on his phone." She hesitated. "I don't think he saw what happened. I guess sometimes he ran errands for her and sometimes he dropped her off at different places so she could do them herself." Rowesa shrugged.

Beatrice asked, "So what did you say to Felton?"

Rowesa sighed. "What could I say, after that? It was totally obvious what I'd done. I just spluttered something out and the whole time Mrs. Billows was looking at me with this awful smirk. She thought she knew the kind of person I was and I couldn't blame her, after what she'd seen. I suddenly just wanted to convince her that I *wasn't* that person—that I'd planned on telling Mrs. Bradwell that I'd made a mistake. That I was going to give her the whole amount."

Wyatt asked, "Did you convince her?"

Rowesa shook her head. "She didn't want to listen to anything I said. She said she should go right over to the police station and talk to Ramsay. I just stood there, shaking. Then she said that she needed my phone number."

Beatrice raised her eyebrows. "Did you ask her why?"

Rowesa shook her head again. "I wasn't even thinking straight. I just took out some paper and a pen and gave it to her."

Wyatt asked, "What happened when you got back to Mrs. Bradwell's house?"

Rowesa said, "I gave her all of the money. I told her I'd made a mistake and that I'd taken out too much. But the thing is, I'm not sure I *would* have done that if Mrs. Billows hadn't witnessed me taking some of it away."

"I'm guessing you received a phone call from Felton Billows at some point," said Beatrice wryly.

"Later that day. She didn't waste much time." Rowesa's voice was bitter. "She told me that she'd not only tell Mrs. Bradwell that I'd divided the money up and put some of it in my pocket, but she'd tell the police if I didn't pay her money."

Wyatt said gently, "That must have been really frightening."

"It was. I felt like she had so much control over me. If I went to jail, who would take care of my daughter? What would we do? I couldn't believe I'd put myself in that situation to begin with—I was so furious with myself."

Beatrice asked, "What did you say to her? Was she asking for a lot of money?"

"It wouldn't sound like a lot of money, but it was a huge amount for me. I told her that was the whole reason I'd been dishonest to begin with—because we didn't even have enough money to pay the electric bill. She wouldn't hear anything about it, though. She just told me if I didn't want to go to jail, that I'd find a way." Rowesa rubbed her forehead as if it hurt.

"Did you pay anything?" asked Beatrice.

"Only a tiny amount of what she was asking for. She wanted a hundred dollars right off the bat and I gave her eight. She really rolled her eyes at that and said that wasn't enough to keep her from telling her old friend that she was being taken advantage of. I told Mrs. Billows that I'd given Mrs. Bradwell the whole amount—that I hadn't stolen any of the money at all. But she wouldn't listen to me. She just kept haranguing me for the money."

They all sat silently for a few moments. And now Felton Billows was dead.

Rowesa took another deep breath. "You probably know what I'm about to say next. Of course, Mrs. Billows is dead and her death is suspicious." Her eyes were wide and full of desperation. "I didn't have *anything* to do with her death. I still feel so guilty about even thinking about taking money from Mrs. Bradwell. I would never be able to live with myself if I actually took another human life. Besides, even though I was upset and mad at Mrs. Billows for blackmailing me, I sort of felt like I brought it on myself because of what I did. But I'm really worried now. I don't know if maybe Mrs. Billows mentioned something about me to someone else or not. I wonder if the police are going to come around and speak with me. If they knew what happened, they'd think I could have been involved in her death so I didn't have to pay her."

Beatrice knew Edith was aware of the argument between Rowesa and Felton. But she wasn't sure it was something Edith would go to the police about.

Wyatt said slowly, "Surely Felton wouldn't have mentioned she was blackmailing you to anyone."

Rowesa shrugged. "Maybe not. Maybe it was more that she told someone that she'd seen me do something suspicious. I don't know—I'm just really jumpy right now and everything seems like it might be possible. That's why I've come here. Well, I'm here for a couple of different reasons. For one, my conscience is so guilty that it's driving me crazy and I needed to talk to someone about it. But for another, I need help figuring out what I should do."

Wyatt and Beatrice glanced quickly at each other. Wyatt said, "Rowesa, I think the most important thing for you to do is to tell Mrs. Bradwell what really happened. I don't think the feeling of guilt is really going to go away until you do."

Rowesa bent her head down and the curtain of hair fell over it for a few moments. Then she lifted her head again. "That's what I thought you might say. And it's what, deep down, I thought I should probably do. The problem is I have so much to lose. Mrs. Bradwell won't be able to trust me after that, and trust is the most important part of the job. She's trusting me to be in her home with her and go to the drugstore for her and run bank errands. How will she be able to trust me again after this? And what if she goes to the police?"

Beatrice said softly, "I think you should speak with the police, too. Ramsay is easy to talk to and it's important that he hears this from you and not from someone else. Because you're right—someone *might* know something about your theft and go to the police. It's better that they hear it from you. And that they hear the whole story—that Felton was blackmailing you. Who knows—if she did it to you, might she have done it to someone else, too?"

Rowesa turned pale. "What if the police think I killed Mrs. Billows? It's one thing if I tell them I intended to take money from Mrs. Bradwell, even though I didn't. It's another if they think I killed Mrs. Billows because I couldn't afford to pay her the blackmail money."

Beatrice said, "Do you have a good alibi for yesterday morning?"

Rowesa shook her head. "I was out running errands for Mrs. Bradwell. As far as the police are concerned, I could have been anywhere: even murdering Mrs. Billows. I mean, they could arrest me. What would happen to Ashley then?"

"You know Ramsay, though; he's always been fair. And the risk of staying silent about this is too high and will make you appear guilty even when you're not," said Beatrice softly.

Rowesa slowly nodded. "It's been hard lately. I've been so distracted when I've been with Ashley. And when I look at her and she's so innocent and thinks I'm so wonderful, I feel so ashamed of myself." She paused and thought for a few minutes. "I think I have to do it. I need to tell Mrs. Bradwell and the police and just see what happens."

Wyatt asked, "Would you like us to go with you when you do? Just to have some support there?"

She gave him a grateful look. "I really appreciate that. But I think this is something I need to face on my own."

Beatrice said, "Did Felton ever mention *why* she was blackmailing you? I mean, it must have been a surprise when she approached you like that."

Rowesa gave a short laugh. "I was totally shocked. I'd always thought Mrs. Billows, who is from one of the oldest families around here, had plenty of money. But she did say that her son, who'd moved back to Dappled Hills was using up her savings. She sounded really upset about it. She was sort of blaming her son for the fact she was blackmailing me. I guess her son isn't in great financial shape, either, if she was having to give him money."

She gave Noo-noo a final, loving rub and stood up. "I don't know how to thank you both for being so generous with your time and with hearing me out. I feel like a huge weight has been lifted from me. Well, I guess it's not *totally* lifted off me, but it's much lighter than it was when I got here. Thank you."

Wyatt and Beatrice stood up. Wyatt said, "That's what we're here for. Please let us know how it goes."

"I will. I'm planning on going straight over to Mrs. Bradwell now and then right to the police station before my courage fails me." She waved to them as she hurried out the door.

Beatrice and Wyatt looked at each other. "That's something else," said Wyatt slowly. "Not necessarily about Rowesa—it's clear she was incredibly desperate to consider doing what she did. But it's pretty shocking to me the role Felton played in all of this."

Beatrice said, "I never really had a good reading on Felton, which is probably my fault since I was avoiding her most of the time. She could be all bubbly like she was yesterday or she could be kind of crafty-looking, like she had all sorts of secrets and something up her sleeve. Clearly she *did* have secrets and something up her sleeve."

"I'm just glad Rowesa is going to tell Lucy Bradwell and Ramsay what happened. That's the only way she was going to be able to live with herself. I could see how horribly guilty she felt," said Wyatt.

Beatrice nodded. "Being proactive is the only way to handle it." She sat down on the sofa. "Like I said, I'm not *totally* shocked that Felton could do something like that. And to me, her crime was much worse than Rowesa's."

"Do you think her financial situation was really that bad?"

Beatrice said, "I don't think it was just the money. To Felton, her reputation and standing in Dappled Hills was everything. I mean, you couldn't have a conversation with her without her saying something about her family or her upbringing. Or flashing her jewelry around."

Wyatt frowned. "And apparently, that diamond ring is missing. So it seems like money must be a motive."

Beatrice sighed. "Which, of course, would also point to Rowesa. But think about it—she had absolutely no need to come by and tell us what she did today. As far as she's concerned, nobody might ever know."

Wyatt said slowly, "Except you mentioned Edith had heard Rowesa and Felton arguing."

"Right. Rowesa didn't know that, though. But she was still worried that somehow people knew about her taking the money and she wasn't far off. I just can't see Rowesa deliberately knocking Felton down the stairs and then taking her ring. It doesn't sound like something she'd be capable of."

Wyatt said, "I didn't think she'd be capable of theft. Although she didn't go through with it."

"I can't wait to hear how her conversation with Mrs. Bradwell and Ramsay goes. I hope she'll get back in touch with us soon," said Beatrice.

The next hour passed quietly. Beatrice took her book out and read for a while and Wyatt took a nap with Noo-noo cuddled up with him on the sofa. When Wyatt's phone chirped, Beatrice put her book down and waited to hear who the text was from.

He pulled out his phone with some difficulty since Noo-noo was still sleeping on him. He squinted at it and then smiled. "Mrs. Bradwell was very understanding and didn't want to press charges."

"I always did like Lucy Bradwell," said Beatrice. "Has Rowesa made it to the police station, too?"

Wyatt frowned at the phone. "It looks like she's typing something now." He paused for a few moments. "She spoke with Ramsay and he asked her a lot of questions about where she was, apparently. But she wasn't arrested. She sounds so relieved." He typed back a response to Rowesa.

There was a tap on the door and Noo-noo gave a few barks and leapt off Wyatt's lap and trotted to the front door. Beatrice opened the door to see Ramsay there.

"Come on in," said Beatrice. "We were just talking about you."

Wyatt stood up and shook Ramsay's hand and Ramsay plopped down in one of the armchairs. He grinned at them. "You've both been mentioned recently, too. I had a visitor this afternoon and apparently you know all about it."

Beatrice said, "Well, we thought it was a good idea for her to speak with you, considering what she told us."

Ramsay nodded. "I'm glad you did. It definitely helps provide us with a clearer picture of Felton Billows, if nothing else. If she's the kind of person who'd blackmail someone else, that opens up another avenue for us to pursue."

Beatrice gave Ramsay an assessing look. "What did you think about Rowesa, though? What did you make of her story?"

Ramsay sighed and leaned down to scratch Noo-noo behind the ears. "I felt sorry for her, truth be told. She seems like the kind of person who *wants* to do the right thing and nothing is really working out for her. So she considered doing something she shouldn't have done and then the wrong person observed her darkest moment. Bad timing."

Wyatt said, "Maybe it counts for something that she came forward and spoke with you? She didn't have to do that, after all. Surely she wouldn't have implicated herself if she was involved in Felton's death in any way."

Ramsay nodded. "True. It does count for something, of course, but it would have been better if Rowesa could have accounted for her movements in some way. She was all over town and sure could have done it. She was feeling very desperate. Maybe the confession was also a way to make her look less-guilty."

Beatrice said, "Ramsay, can I get you a sandwich or something to drink? I was so interested in hearing what you had to say that I forgot to even ask."

Ramsay gave her a grateful grin. "Could you? Today has been crazy and I haven't had the time to grab anything to eat. I'd have gone home before I head back out, but Meadow has the baby and she'd have held me up for over an hour showing me two hundred pictures of all the cute things Will had done while he was there."

"That sounds very likely." Beatrice chuckled as she headed into the kitchen to put together a couple of sandwiches and an iced tea.

He took them from her a few minutes later. "You're the best, Beatrice. Thanks."

"You're welcome. Although I will add that Will *does do* a lot of really cute things." Beatrice's eyes twinkled impishly.

He held up his hands, "Oh, I know, I know! Believe me, I'm definitely a member of the Will fan club. But right now, I just don't have the time to get sucked into seeing today's batch of photos and videos."

"Videos, too?" asked Wyatt wryly.

"Oh, heavens yes! Video after video. I'm sure Meadow is about to lose space on her phone. Actually, I'm waiting for that moment."

Ramsay asked them how they were doing, likely a ploy to eat as quickly as possible without speaking with his mouth full. They both obediently recited information about the guild meeting and happenings at the church while he quickly polished off his sandwiches and tea.

Then Ramsay sighed and patted his generous stomach. "That was very good, Beatrice, thank you."

"High praise coming from someone who gets to eat Meadow's home cooking on a daily basis," said Beatrice teasingly.

Ramsay said, "Well, believe me, it hit the spot. I guess I'll have to head back out to it." He pulled a face. Policing, although it was his chosen profession, was never Ramsay's first love. Instead, he'd rather be reading or writing his own creative pieces.

"How's it going?" asked Beatrice, trying not to sound too nosy.

He sighed. "I'm not sure. I guess by now I don't even have to say that her death *was* a result of murder?" He looked at them and could tell they'd already heard that bit of information else-where. "Small towns. I figured. The missing ring is kind of weird. I don't know what to make of that. Either someone actually *had* a financial motive for the crime, or else someone wanted us to *think* there was a financial motive for the crime. And then there's Lucius." He shook his head.

Beatrice's ears pricked up. "Lucius Craft?" Lucius was a gre-garious man who loved literature and talking about books with both Ramsay and Beatrice. In fact, they'd gotten many tips about good things to read from him.

Ramsay nodded. "Our friend and fellow reader."

Wyatt frowned. "What's been going on with Lucius? Did he know Felton?"

Ramsay said, "He did, although it didn't sound as though he knew her extremely well. But apparently, he'd always listen to her stories about her childhood."

Beatrice said, "I'd never put the two of them together as be-ing friends."

"I'm not sure they were friends, but definitely acquain-tances. Anyway, Lucius was pretty generous with his time in terms of listening to her stories, which may have encouraged her to make them even more exaggerated. Then there's the kick-er—Lucius was found breaking into the jewelry shop down-town last night." He gave a wry smile at Wyatt and Beatrice's wide-eyed reaction.

Chapter Ten

Ramsay continued, "That's right. I was just as surprised as you were. An alarm went off and I happened to be very close by and was able to nab him quickly. Since he's only been a resident of Dappled Hills for the last seven years, I ran his fingerprints out of curiosity. Came to find out that he has other names and crimes in several states."

"Crimes?" asked Beatrice. She had a hard time squaring what Ramsay was telling her with what she knew of the somewhat professorial-looking older man she'd come to know.

"Same sort of thing. Nothing violent, no drugs, nothing like that. But quite a bit of breaking and entering. Theft. He's mostly focused on jewelry, although he apparently dabbled in art thievery some time ago."

Wyatt shook his head. "And this happened while your investigation is going on. No wonder you haven't had any time to eat."

Ramsay said, "That's the thing—Lucius planned it that way. He figured I'd be so caught up with the murder investigation that I'd not be able to get to the jewelry store in time to catch him."

"How was he when you *did* arrest him?" asked Beatrice curiously. "I'm still having a tough time picturing him as a thief."

"Oh, he was very apologetic and kind of abashed. Like I'd caught him out using bad table manners instead of robbing a store."

Wyatt asked, "Where is he now? Is he in the Dappled Hills jail or has he been sent off to another county facility?"

Ramsay rubbed his face. "He's here for now in our holding cells so I can question him about Felton's death. But he's wanted for crimes in other states, so eventually he'll be leaving Dappled Hills to face those charges."

"Is he able to have visitors?" asked Wyatt.

Ramsay nodded his head. "You know our jail set-up. He'll have to be in the pen, but you can come sign in at the desk and speak with him. He'd probably really appreciate a visit from you and Beatrice, too. Maybe that would make him relaxed enough to answer the questions I have, too."

Beatrice said, "But in all the crimes you saw, you didn't see anything violent on his record."

"That's right."

"So doesn't it seem really unlikely that Lucius would have murdered Felton?" asked Beatrice.

Ramsay sighed. "We just don't know what might have happened. Maybe he thought Felton was safely out gardening and slipped into her house to take some of the jewelry and that tiara she was always talking about. Then maybe she quietly came back inside, caught him in the act, and he was put in the position of either getting rid of Felton or being arrested."

"But what happened to the jewelry?" asked Wyatt. "Did Lucius say anything about Felton's diamond ring?"

"All he said was that he had nothing to do with the theft at her house or her murder. He denies everything." Ramsay shook his head. "This has been a pretty convoluted case so far. I'd really like to wrap it up soon. For one thing, there's a murderer out there who could strike again. For another and more selfish reason, I had a project I was working on before this case started."

Beatrice smiled. "I hope you're going to say you've been writing again."

Wyatt asked, "More poetry?"

"Not this time. Oh, I like writing poetry well enough, but the problem is doing anything with it. It's not like I have enough to publish and book of poetry. I'm still writing some for my own enjoyment, but I've moved back over to short story writing. You know I was doing that a while back, Beatrice."

She nodded. "Good to hear you're picking it back up again, even if you're having to take an unexpected break. I'd love to read it if you are letting people take a look."

Ramsay's face lit up. "Would you? I'd really like to have your opinion on it. Yours too, Wyatt, if you have the chance. I wondered if a couple of them might be good enough to submit to an anthology or a contest or a literary magazine or something." He blushed a little. "I'm not saying that they *are*, mind you, just that I'd like to see if they might be."

"Well, I'd love to take a look. Do you have them where you can email them to us?" asked Beatrice.

Ramsay grinned. "Even better . . . I'd printed them out and stuck them in a notebook of mine in the car. Let me run get them."

He was back a moment later, opening a battered notebook and taking out a few printed sheets of paper. "I don't want to overwhelm y'all with this stuff, so I'll just hand you a couple for starters. These are my favorites, anyway. Besides, I know you're both reading books, anyhow. What *are* you reading, by the way?"

Wyatt said, "Actually, I'm between books right now, but I might start reading the book Beatrice is reading when she's done."

"It's really good, Ramsay. I think you'd like it. It's a mystery." Beatrice's eyes twinkled.

Ramsay groaned. "I don't know if I can handle a mystery after dealing with this one."

"No, this isn't just a straightforward mystery—it's really a lot of fun, especially the characters. The sleuth is a young girl. It's called *The Sweetness at the Bottom of the Pie* by Alan Bradley. You should give it a go."

Ramsay said, "Maybe after all this gets wrapped up. Thanks, Beatrice. And thanks for reading the stories."

The next morning, Wyatt and Beatrice were having coffee when Wyatt asked, "What do you think about going to the police station to see Lucius?"

"Absolutely," said Beatrice immediately. "I've always enjoyed spending time with him and he's been nothing but kind and pleasant to me. I'm totally shocked that he apparently has this whole other side."

Wyatt said, "He might be a little uncomfortable about seeing us, but I think showing him that we're concerned about him is worth a little embarrassment on his end, don't you think?"

Beatrice nodded. "I think it would be very lonely in the local jail. There's likely no one else locked up in there and there's probably just a sole deputy who checks in on Lucius from time to time."

After they ate breakfast and quickly walked Noo-noo, they headed over to the small police station that was part of the Dappled Hills town hall. Beatrice had at first thought she'd bring something for Lucius to eat but called Ramsay first to check and found it was against the rules.

There was a young deputy on duty, looking at his phone and seemingly extremely bored when they arrived. He perked up when Wyatt and Beatrice came in.

"Sure, you can visit with him. He's going to have to stay in his cell, though, since we don't have a visitor room. I can pull a couple of folding chairs in there for you, so you can sit down. Just sign the log right here." He pushed over a very empty visitor log.

The deputy picked up the folding chairs and pushed his foot against a heavy door that led to the back room of the station. There was Lucius, looking very out of place in the cell. He was a handsome older man with silver hair and a twinkle in his eyes . . . a twinkle that Beatrice was glad to see was still there.

"My friends!" said Lucius, giving them both a warm smile. "I can't tell you how much it warms my old heart to see you both here. I only wish we could be visiting in slightly different circumstances."

Wyatt smiled back at him. "I'm wishing the same thing, Lucius. Are you doing all right in here?"

Lucius gave a chuckle. "Actually, I'm very well-treated in here. I don't think Dappled Hills has many people enter their cells. This one seems practically brand-new and sparkles with cleanliness. You should see some of the other places I've been incarcerated in."

Beatrice shuddered and Lucius added, "Or maybe not! You wouldn't be impressed, I assure you. But here they check in with me frequently and have even brought me my favorite fast food choices from time to time. It's a nice set-up and a pity I likely won't be here long before I'm shipped off elsewhere."

Beatrice said with a frown, "So you're facing charges in other states, is that right?"

Lucius gave her a rueful look. "I'm afraid so. So you see, this is my own doing and you shouldn't feel too badly for me. I suppose they'll be sending me off to whatever state has the most to charge me with."

Beatrice said, "But how did this all happen? When did it start?" She stopped and then said, "Sorry for all the questions. But I was so bowled over when Ramsay told me. Wyatt and I know you as a totally different person. You're always so suave and sophisticated and enjoy literature and good music."

"And I *am* a totally different person. But I also have this other side of me that likes the thrill of . . . well, of that sort of life, I guess. And, to answer your question, it all started when I was very young. My grandfather raised me and he was, to put it bluntly, a con man. He was charming and fun to be around and he'd become close with someone and then completely betray their confidence while taking their money at the same time."

Wyatt asked slowly, "Did he get caught? What would have happened to you when he was incarcerated?"

Lucius said airily, "Oh, I suppose I would have been in some sort of foster care or a group home or something. But the thing is, he never was. We just kept moving, never in the same town more than a few months. He'd win people over in every town we moved to and the pattern repeated. But I never followed in his footsteps in terms of becoming a con man. I felt like he left this human trail of misery behind him. He victimized so many people and I doubt many of them even reported his crimes because they were ashamed of having been so gullible."

"So you were looking for more of a victimless crime?" asked Beatrice.

Lucius nodded and gave her a smile. "That's right. Although that's not to say that my crimes *are* victimless, just that they're not as directly personal and hurtful as the crimes my grandfather perpetrated. That doesn't mean that I'm not deeply ashamed that you've seen me at this low point."

Wyatt said, "We wanted to let you know we're thinking about you. You're our friend, Lucius."

Beatrice nodded. Lucius smiled at her. "I have a feeling you still have some questions about me, Beatrice. Which I completely understand."

"Is it solely for the money? I mean, when you're breaking into businesses. For some reason, I'd always had the impression that you were fairly comfortable," said Beatrice.

Lucius sighed. "That's the thing—I *am* fairly comfortable, although it's off of ill-gotten gains, either from what I've purloined or from my grandfather's estate that I inherited. No, I'm afraid the truth is that I enjoy the thrill of it all to a certain extent. So there you are. I'm no Robin Hood, Beatrice, if that's what you were wondering."

"And Ramsay has been asking you about Felton's death," said Beatrice with a frown. "Is that just because of what he'd found out about you?"

Lucius gave an elegant shrug. "Think of it from Ramsay's perspective. He's had this terrible murder happen. He believes an expensive ring and possibly other jewelry is stolen. This is an unusual event in Dappled Hills. Then he happens to nab someone breaking into a jewelry store downtown. He runs the fingerprints and *voila*! He's discovered a career thief and one who specializes in jewelry. I know the last thing Ramsay wants to do is run police investigations because he'd rather be reading some wonderful book or writing his stories and poems. Of course, he'd like to believe he can wrap the case up this easily."

Wyatt said gently, "But he can't, can he?"

Lucius shook his head. "I'm afraid he can't. I wasn't over at Felton's house when she died. That's because I was taking money from a cash register at a local consignment business at the time while an employee was otherwise distracted. Besides, I wouldn't have been interested in Felton's jewelry."

Beatrice lifted her eyebrows. "Why is that?"

Lucius shrugged again. "Because they were fakes. I've known that since I've lived here."

Beatrice and Wyatt stared at him.

Lucius chuckled at their expressions. "That's right. I could tell right off the bat that Felton was some sort of fantasist. Believe me, after growing up with my grandfather, I know when someone is spinning a tall tale. Felton's were quite extraordinary. I have to wonder why she felt the need to come up with something that huge when she could just as easily have made up a simpler story."

Wyatt asked, "Why do you think she did?"

Lucius leaned back on the wall in his cell. "Well, I've devoted some time considering this very point. I think it's because it was the only way she could think of to make people love her. She wanted to stand out and bring people in. So she came up with a huge story in the hopes she would draw friends in. But all she did for the most part was to draw in a sycophant."

"You mean Edith," said Beatrice.

Lucius nodded. "You've noticed, too. Yes, Edith seemed completely wide-eyed and amazed with her stories. When I'd see Felton and Edith together, it looked like Edith *felt* special because she thought *Felton* was special. But Beatrice, I have the feeling you didn't feel exactly the same way about Felton's stories. I'd like to hear how you looked at them."

Beatrice blew out a sigh. "Well, it sounds terrible to say, but I found her stories very annoying."

Lucius laughed. "That's what I thought you'd say. So you likely avoided her company so you didn't have to hear the incessant stories."

"That's right," admitted Beatrice.

"She was actually driving you *away* with her stories, instead of drawing you in. And I think many people in town felt the same way. It sounded like bragging."

Beatrice said, "Exactly. It wasn't that I didn't believe her. In fact, I *did* believe her. But I didn't want to hear any more about her upbringing and the tiara she had and all the rest of it."

"And, consequently, she would tell you *more* about it all. Because what she was doing wasn't working on you and she thought the only way to draw you in was to talk *more* about it," said Lucius.

"A vicious cycle," said Beatrice ruefully.

Lucius said, "But I could tell with Edith that Felton's stories made her feel *special*. Special to be picked out by someone like Felton to spend time with."

Wyatt said, "How did you know the jewels were fakes?"

Lucius said, "Oh, I have an eye for that kind of thing. I'm a cat burglar, right? I know the quality of jewelry when I see it. And some art, too, although art can be harder. Anyway, when I first moved here, I was very interested in Felton as sort of a psychological study in a way. What made her tick? Why was she so determined to perpetuate these stories of hers? I suppose I might have fawned over her a little just to see if I could find out why she behaved the way she did. She was out one morning with Edith in downtown Dappled Hills and they came right over to speak with me while I did my best to be charming. I made some sort of polite comment about her ring and she lay her hand right on top of mine so I could see it up close."

Beatrice said, "Could you tell right away it was a fake?"

"Certainly. It was paste, although it was an excellent piece of costume jewelry. She might have paid a pretty penny for it. But it definitely wasn't old and definitely wasn't real. And the entire time I was appraising it, Edith was bouncing around like Tigger from *Winnie the Pooh* and asking if I'd ever seen a prettier ring. And then going on and on about how Felton had a tiara in her bedroom and all sorts of other jewels. Felton just stood there and preened."

Wyatt asked, "Did you tell Felton you knew it wasn't real?"

Lucius snorted. "No. It's not my place to make someone else look completely ridiculous. I mean, to me Felton already seemed that way because I knew it wasn't real."

Beatrice said, "Do you think anyone else would be able to tell at a glance that Felton's jewelry was fake?"

Lucius shook his head. "I doubt it. Oh, I have no doubt the local jeweler would be able to tell immediately that it wasn't real, but I have the feeling Felton, if she went to the jewelry shop at all, would be sure not to wear her ring in there. She struck me as the kind of woman who wouldn't want to be exposed that way."

"You know it's missing," said Beatrice. "Felton's ring, that is."

Lucius shook his head. "All I can say is it's a terrible tragedy if Felton Billows was murdered over her fake jewelry. She shouldn't have been making up stories about herself and she shouldn't have bragged about her ring and other things. But she didn't deserve to die over them, that's for sure."

"Have you told Ramsay that you knew the jewelry wasn't real?" asked Wyatt.

"Not yet. We really haven't had a chance to chat much. He was busily finding out about my criminal past and then working on Felton's murder. I just told him I wasn't involved in her death. But I'll let him know as soon as he comes back. As you can imagine, jewelry aside, I had no reason to murder Felton."

Beatrice asked, "Could you think of anyone who *did* have a motive? We're in such a small town that it's easy to hear things or observe things sometimes. And you seem to be astute when it comes to reading people."

Lucius laughed. "Only because reading people is an important part of my job. And yes, I have made a few observations. One was that Felton wasn't very nice to her son. Rupert, isn't it? I heard her berating him over some trivial thing the other day. I don't think it made him very pleased. I also noticed he seemed very short on cash. Being short on cash is a very stressful situation and different people respond in different ways."

"How would you guess Rupert might respond?" asked Beatrice.

"It's anybody's guess, but mine would be that he might be a little dangerous. He doesn't seem like a man who's been short on cash often. And he doesn't seem like a man who would be grateful for handouts, such as he was getting from his mother. And I don't believe he'd have taken kindly to her telling everyone how she was supporting him. I'm not saying that he killed his mother, mind you, only that it could be a possible reaction to the stress he was under. Maybe he didn't even intend to do it. Maybe he couldn't help himself from finally lashing out when the straw broke the camel's back." Lucius shrugged.

"Anyone else?" asked Beatrice.

Lucius sighed. "I hate to speak ill of the young and I know Felton always spoke highly of her teenaged employee. But I can tell the boy has some issues."

"Haskell?" asked Wyatt.

"That's the one." Lucius shook his head. "I'm afraid that one is heading into some trouble. I've seen some of the boys he's hanging around with, and they're *definitely* trouble. Besides, something in his expression the other day made me think he might be experimenting with drugs. He had a rather vacant stare and bloodshot eyes."

Wyatt and Beatrice exchanged glances. Betty would be devastated if that were true.

Lucius added, "I'm not saying he's responsible for Felton's death, but it makes you wonder. If his new, inappropriate friends really needed a fix and were low on cash, would they persuade him to steal from his employer?"

The young deputy came through the heavy door. "Time's up," he announced.

Lucius politely stood. "I'm so happy you came by."

Wyatt and Beatrice stood too, and gave him a smile. "Thanks for seeing us. We'll try to come by again soon," said Beatrice.

Chapter Eleven

They walked out into the lobby, signed out on the visitor's log, and walked outside. Wyatt said, "He's still the same Lucius, isn't he? Despite having this other side to him."

"Just as pleasant as ever," agreed Beatrice. "We could have been in there discussing books and he'd have had the same manner. I don't think that part of him is a sham at all. After all, he has nothing to gain by being nice to us now."

Wyatt nodded. "What do you make of what he was saying about Felton?"

"It sounds as if he was supremely well-qualified to be able to see through her. After all, he's built up his own persona. And he apparently has an expertise when it comes to jewelry. I'm definitely surprised that Felton wasn't who she said she was, but I'm not quite as shocked as I thought I'd be."

"Why is that?" asked Wyatt.

"Maybe because she just went on and on about her background and her money. Most people who come from that type of life don't usually harp on it, do they? Maybe, on some level, I realized she wasn't everything she appeared."

"And Rupert?" asked Wyatt.

"Maybe Rupert is capable of more than we thought. I'm not saying he's responsible, but he must have been furious at the way his mother was treating him. Maybe it's as Lucius said: he'd finally had enough one day."

They got into the car and headed from downtown to home. Beatrice frowned, staring out the passenger window. "Wait—are those emergency vehicles over at Felton's again?"

Wyatt slowed down. "No, I think they're at Rupert's."

"Should we go there?" asked Beatrice.

Wyatt nodded. "Let's just check and see if Rupert needs help. With his mother gone, he doesn't really have anyone in town to rely on."

Wyatt carefully pulled the car off the street and out of the way of the police cars and ambulance. There looked to be state police there, too.

Beatrice frowned at the scene as they got out of the car. "This doesn't look good."

Wyatt said, "Ramsay's coming over to talk to us."

Ramsay had spotted them and was swiftly walking over, a grim look on his face. "Were you here to speak with Rupert?"

Wyatt shook his head. "Only when we saw all the cars. We thought we should check up on him."

Ramsay blew out a sigh. "I'm afraid there's no need to check in at this point. He's gone. Murdered at what appears to be sometime earlier today. I'd run by to talk to him about his mom and found him dead."

Beatrice and Wyatt stared at him.

"Have you been in touch with him recently?" asked Ramsay.

"We visited him yesterday," said Wyatt. "Beatrice and I brought over food and we spoke about his mother's service for a little while."

"Did he mention anything else? Any worries? Anything on his mind? Any thoughts about what may have happened to his mother?"

Beatrice said, "He opened up in some ways, but didn't tell us about feeling threatened in any way. He wasn't happy about being back home, of course, or getting assistance from his mom. He was upset about the financial situation—both his, and his mother's. He'd thought Felton would have had more of an estate to leave him."

Ramsay shook his head. "Judging from the bareness of his house, he sure didn't seem to have much. Did he mention anything about Rowesa Fant while you were there?" asked Ramsay.

Wyatt said, "He didn't seem to know anything about her."

Ramsay was quiet for a moment and Beatrice said, "Why . . . do you think he was planning on blackmailing Rowesa where his mother left off?"

Ramsay rubbed his face. "I just don't know. It would make sense, wouldn't it? Rupert was in terrible financial straits from what he's said and from what we've been able to gather. It would have been easy enough for him to have continued blackmailing Rowesa. He wouldn't have known that she'd already spoken to her employer and the police."

"But why would Rowesa kill him? After all, she's already confessed, as you've just mentioned. What possible reason would she have to murder Rupert?" asked Beatrice.

Ramsay shrugged, a tired look on his face. "I don't know. None of this is making sense to me right now and I'm not sure if it's because I'm exhausted or because it's genuinely baffling. Maybe he knew something else about Rowesa. Maybe he realized she *did* murder his mother. After all, this house is very close to Felton's. He could have seen Rowesa slip over there and see her run off afterwards. Maybe he thought it would be a good opportunity for him to make a little money while he's trying to find a job. Then Rowesa killed Rupert when she realized he knew her secret."

Beatrice said, "I don't know. Swiping extra money at the ATM is one thing, but murdering two people in cold blood is something completely different. I just have a hard time picturing Rowesa doing something like this."

Ramsay said, "Can you keep this under your hats?" They nodded and he added, "And be sure not to tell Meadow. You know she can't keep a secret to save her own life. Anyway, it was the kind of murder that anyone could have done—it wouldn't have taken a lot of strength. It looks like hot coffee was thrown at his face as a distraction and then he was hit over the head with a rolling pin."

"A rolling pin?" asked Beatrice.

"That's right," said Ramsay. "Why?"

"Just that his house wasn't exactly well-equipped. There wasn't even a place for us to sit down. And I find it hard to believe that Rupert would have had rolling pins lying around."

Ramsay nodded thoughtfully. "It was pretty barren in there. Maybe the killer brought it in with them, who knows? At any rate, there are no fingerprints, so they thought to wipe them off."

He glanced up at the sound of a motor and Wyatt and Beatrice turned to see Felton's yardman, Devlin Harley, pulling up to the house. Ramsay frowned. "This guy always seems to turn up at bad times."

As Devlin nonchalantly hopped out of his truck and started removing yard equipment, Beatrice added, "And he never seems to realize it might be a bad time to mow the grass."

Ramsay strode over to Devlin, "Hey, you can't be on the property now."

"Here to mow," said Devlin laconically.

"Not right now, you're not." Ramsay pointed at the back of Devlin's truck. "Put that stuff back up and head off to your next job."

While Ramsay spoke with Devlin, Chrissy Jo from the guild meeting walked up to join them with a concerned expression on her face.

"What's happening?" she asked a little breathlessly. "I saw all the emergency vehicles."

Beatrice told her and Chrissy Jo's face fell. "Felton first and now her son?" She shook her head as if she couldn't believe it. "I was planning on seeing Edith but she wasn't in, so I just continued my walk. I saw Ramsay's car pull up, but didn't think anything of it until now."

Wyatt and Chrissy Jo knew each other from when she'd lived in town, and he asked after her family and how she'd been doing.

After Chrissy Jo explained why she was in town, Beatrice said, "I haven't seen any texts from you about your aunt's things."

Chrissy Jo flushed a little. "Oh, I don't know. I took a couple of pictures and then I wondered why on earth I was bothering you with them. I think there may be a few things my aunt owns that are treasures to her family, but not to anyone else."

"Could I see your pictures?" asked Beatrice.

Chrissy Jo pulled her phone out and opened up her photo gallery, handing the phone to Beatrice reluctantly.

Beatrice looked at the photos carefully, taking special interest in one and blowing it up to study it.

Wyatt said, "What do you think?"

Beatrice cleared her throat. "I think Chrissy Jo is right about the doll collection. These dolls are old, but not really collectible since they're still pretty readily available online. Plus, they've been well-loved, too."

Chrissy Jo nodded and gave her an apologetic look. "Sorry for wasting your time with this."

Beatrice shook her head. "It wasn't a waste at all. I saw two interesting things in the background of the pictures. One was a rug that I'd like to take a closer look at. The other was a collection of duck decoys."

Chrissy Jo stared at her. "You're kidding. The duck decoys might be worth something?"

"They're very collectible right now. And the rug, which is in good condition, needs someone to take a look at it. I have a couple of friends who are appraisers who could take a look if you could take a few photos that zoom in on the rug and the decoys."

"You don't think they'd mind?" asked Chrissy Jo hesitantly.

"Oh, they live for that kind of thing. They love making these kinds of discoveries. Of course, I don't *know* these items are worth much because I specialized in other areas, but I'd really like them to take a look and see what they think."

Chrissy Jo beamed. "I'll take the pictures and send them over right when I get home. Thanks for this, Beatrice."

As Chrissy Jo took her leave, a police officer called out to Ramsay, still speaking with Devlin, and Ramsay walked off to join the other officers in the house. Devlin loped over to where Wyatt and Beatrice were standing.

"What's going on now?" he asked them, staring at Rupert's house.

Beatrice said, "Rupert Billows is dead."

Devlin's eyes opened wide. "What, him, too?" He shook his head. "Somebody's got it in for that family."

Wyatt asked, "Was Rupert having you take care of his lawn, too?"

Devlin nodded. "Yep. When his mom died, he called up and said he'd take care of the back-pay his mom owed me if I'd still keep up her yard and his, too."

Beatrice asked, "Did he? Pay you, I mean?"

"He did. He was right decent about it. Paid me the back-pay, paid me upfront for doing his yard, and even gave a little extra for the inconvenience, he said." He scowled at the house. "Now I guess I'm not getting any more."

Beatrice asked, "What have you been up to this morning so far?"

Devlin shrugged. "Sleeping. Then working. I work hard and I sleep hard. Got a bit of a later start this morning, seeing as how I was extra tired."

Beatrice said, "There's really not a nice way to ask this, but someone was saying you and Felton had been arguing with each other."

Devlin raised a single eyebrow. "That so? Must be that kid."

"Which kid?" asked Wyatt.

"That Haskell. Betty's kid." When he said Betty's name, a faint flush rose over his face. "He's got it in for me."

Beatrice frowned. "Why is that?"

Devlin sighed. "Don't be spreading this across town, but I might be starting to see his mom. You know—going out to the movies and to dinner and such."

"You're dating Betty Lamar?" asked Beatrice.

Devlin scowled again, this time directed at Beatrice. With great dignity he said, "We're starting to go out and do things together, that's all. Don't think the kid likes that much."

Wyatt smiled at him reassuringly. "That's really great, Devlin. How did you two meet?"

Devlin gave him a smile back. "Well, she came by Mrs. Billows's house a couple of times to talk to Haskell when I was over there. She was telling me the same thing you were—that I should visit the church and whatnot. She said she was pretty involved there."

Wyatt nodded. "She sure is. She helps out with lots of different things. I don't know what we'd do without her."

"Anyway, that's how we met. Like I said, I think her son isn't too happy about it. Guess he's used to being the only man around the house." Devlin sighed. "I'm not really crazy about the kid myself, but I'm trying to get to know him better. He's right, too—I did argue with Mrs. Billows, but I had a right to be upset. She hadn't paid me for weeks and was always coming up with some sort of lame excuse. But that doesn't mean that I *killed* the lady. I was just annoyed; I wasn't in some kind of psychotic rage or something. Besides, that would be a stupid way to get myself paid, wouldn't it?"

Beatrice and Wyatt nodded their agreement and Devlin continued, "And now Mrs. Billows's son is dead and I guess the cops will come asking questions about him, too. But why would I kill *him*? He's the only one who'd been decent enough to actually pay me."

He rubbed his face with his hands and then looked earnestly at Wyatt. "Look, I'm trying to do better. I'm not saying I've ever been a bad guy, but I don't think I've ever been a really great one, either. I sure haven't been going around following the silver rule." He frowned questioningly. "Silver rule? Isn't that it?"

"Golden rule?" asked Wyatt.

"That's it. So I haven't exactly been a model citizen all the time, but I haven't been breaking laws, either. It's time to do better, though. I'm ready to make my mom proud and maybe even start seeing Betty Lamar and feel like I'm a good enough guy to be her date for things." He peered at Wyatt. "You got any ideas how I should go about that?"

Wyatt said, "Well, if you're looking for ways to get involved in the community, there are plenty of opportunities for that."

Devlin frowned. "Involved—you don't mean like being on the town council or anything."

"No, no, nothing like politics. I meant more in terms of volunteering. Getting out in the community by helping others," said Wyatt.

Devlin brightened at this. "Now that's a good idea. I think that's what Betty spends most of her free time doing, too."

Beatrice said, "I see her at the church all the time. She helps out with the bereavement committee and makes meals for us to deliver to shut-ins and others who need help. She sorts clothes for the clothing ministry. She could probably really be a resource for you if you're trying to find ways to help out. I'm sure she'd have plenty of ideas."

Wyatt added, "We can always use an extra set of hands, too. You'd be really serving the community."

Devlin smiled faintly at this as if it were a new way of looking at himself. Then he sighed as he looked back over at the police working on and around the house. Ramsay was heading back over to them, looking as if he wanted a word with Devlin. "Here come the questions."

Ramsay said, "Before you head out, I'd like to talk with you for a few minutes." He frowned at the yard equipment still scattered around Devlin's feet. "Here, let's put this stuff away before somebody trips over it." He grabbed a string trimmer and Devlin reluctantly picked up his blower.

Ramsay was shoving the trimmer on the back of Devlin's truck when he stopped cold. He pulled a handkerchief out of his pocket and reached forward, grabbing something out of the back of the truck.

"What you got there?" asked Devlin suspiciously.

Ramsay held out his hand. "You tell me," he said in a grim voice.

Beatrice could see it from where she stood. It was Felton's ring.

Chapter Twelve

Devlin backed away as if the ring was a snake.

Ramsay said, "Can you tell me how Felton Billows's ring ended up in your truck?"

"I can't. I don't have anything to do with that thing being there. What use do I have for a diamond ring?" Devlin's eyes narrowed.

Ramsay said, "Well, I didn't think you'd want to wear it, Devlin. But maybe you were looking to sell it. Something like this, you might have thought could bring in a good deal of money. Besides, Felton owed you backpay. Maybe you thought this was one way of getting your money."

Devlin didn't seem to have any idea of the true value of the ring. "She didn't owe me *that* much money. Wouldn't have been right."

Ramsay asked, "When was the last time you saw this ring?"

Devlin was starting to perspire. "I don't know. Whenever she had it on, I guess. I didn't pay much attention to it since she was always wearing it. It wasn't like she just pulled it on for special occasions, you know. I never thought about it one way or another."

"But you knew right away it was hers," said Ramsay quickly.

"Yeah, sure. Because she was always waving it under everybody's noses. That's just the way Mrs. Billows was." He shrugged.

"And you have no idea what it was doing on the back of your truck?"

Devlin gave a short laugh. "Why would I put it there, even if I *did* take it? With all the yard debris and the tools? Where somebody could find it? What kind of stupid person would do something like that?"

Ramsay said again, "You tell me. Seems like the way it must have gotten there is because you put it there for some reason."

Devlin put his hands on his hips. "Maybe *you* put it there. I sure didn't see it there this morning when I was loading up the truck. Maybe you planted it there so you could finally get this murder solved. Makes it real convenient for you, doesn't it?"

Ramsay's face turned thunderous. "Devlin, you've known me your whole life. Have you ever heard of me planting evidence or doing anything unethical?"

Devlin still looked accusingly at him but then slowly his face relaxed. He looked down at the ground and shook his head. He growled, "It has to have gotten there somehow, though. If you didn't do it, somebody else did."

Ramsay sighed. "Devlin, I hate to do this, but I'm going to have to talk to you down at the station about this. Can you just wait in the cruiser for me?"

Devlin's face turned white, then red. "What do you mean? Look, everybody's going to think I did it and I didn't have anything to do with these murders."

Ramsay said, "But you have an important piece of evidence on you."

"On my *truck*."

"Whatever. On your property, how about that? This doesn't have to be a big deal, but I'm going to need a signed statement from you. Just have a seat in the car and we'll head over there with one of the guys from the state police, okay?"

"What about my truck? And all my stuff?" asked Devlin, looking stubborn.

Ramsay rolled his eyes. "It's fine where it is. Do you think anybody is going to be insane enough to steal something in broad daylight when there are this many cops around?"

One of the cops called Ramsay over again and he hurried off.

"I can't believe this," muttered Devlin to Beatrice and Wyatt.

Wyatt said, "Everything is going to be fine. Just tell the truth."

"Yeah, but they obviously don't believe it's the truth." He frowned, looking behind Beatrice. "Great. Now that Edith woman is coming. She'll blab about this all over town. I never did like her."

Beatrice said, "If you go ahead and get in Ramsay's car, she probably won't even notice you. There's a ton of people here."

So Devlin hurried into the police cruiser as Edith came up, staring wide eyed at all the emergency vehicles, most with their lights still going. When she spotted Beatrice and Wyatt, she trotted over. Her face was as white as her hair and she was squeezing her hands together anxiously.

"What's happening?" she asked, grasping onto Beatrice's sleeve. "Is it Felton's son? Is he ill?"

Edith's grip, in her alarm, was especially tight and Beatrice pulled gently away. "It's Rupert, yes. I'm afraid he's dead."

"Dead!" Edith gasped the word. "What—did he have a heart attack, or something? He always did seem sort of wound-up to me. Not in a *bad* way," she hurried to add, as if hating to speak ill of the dead. "But you know . . . he was uptight. And I know he was worried about money because Felton said he was. He was always asking her for help. So was that it? Was it the stress?"

Wyatt shook his head and said gently, "I'm sorry, Edith. I understand that Rupert's death wasn't a natural one."

Edith clasped and unclasped her hands and, if possible, grew even paler. "You don't mean he was *murdered*?"

Beatrice and Wyatt nodded solemnly.

Edith put her hands to her chest. "Oh, *no*. Not Rupert, too. What is *happening*?"

Edith swayed slightly and Wyatt reached out to clasp her elbow. "Let's find a place to sit down, Edith."

Beatrice glanced around. "There's not really a good spot here unless Edith wants to sit in our car."

Edith seemed to come around a little bit. "Let's go back to my house since we're practically there already. We'll just be in the way here. And I could use a glass of water."

Edith started walking shakily away and Wyatt and Beatrice followed.

Edith lived in a cheerful white cottage with ivy growing up the front. She had a small yard that she clearly loved and spent a lot of time in since it was meticulously weeded and upkept. She also had some rather whimsical yard art in the front yard and a white cat stared imperiously at them through a window.

"That's Coco," said Edith, cheering a little at the sight of the cat.

"Cocoa? Like hot chocolate?" asked Beatrice, looking again at the decidedly white fur of the cat.

Edith laughed. "It's Coco, short for coconut." She carefully unlocked the door and pushed it open.

The house was very tidy and cozy with everything in its place. Despite the presence of the cat, Beatrice didn't see a bit of white fur anywhere. There were cheerful red and yellow curtains hanging in the window, a woven rug on the hardwood floor, and candles scattered around on different tables.

Edith led them into the kitchen, which was also sparkling clean with not even a coffee cup in the sink. There was evidence of baking everywhere, from the smell of cookies, to the glass cookie jars full of various goodies.

Edith saw Beatrice looking at the jars. She gave a slightly embarrassed laugh. "I hope you'll have some cookies and some-thing to drink. I obviously can't eat all these." She patted her generous tummy. "When I get stressed out, I like to bake. It gives my hands something to do and calms me down."

"I'd love a cookie," said Wyatt with a smile.

Beatrice nodded. "I would, too."

Edith beamed at them. "How about several? They're good, I promise. You'd think with everything on my mind that I'd end up using salt instead of sugar or something, but I was somehow able to focus on the baking. And I sampled each one, myself."

They took her up on her offer and they were soon munching on cookies and drinking milk. Edith, as she'd mentioned, stuck with water. Wyatt started a casual conversation and soon Edith seemed to be back to normal again.

When they'd finished their cookies and milk, Edith paused and gave them an anxious, fearful look. "Can you tell me what happened?"

Beatrice answered this with a question of her own. "Did you happen to notice anything unusual this morning?"

Focusing on what she'd been doing seemed to make Edith a bit calmer again. "Let's see." Her face wrinkled up with the effort of remembering. "Oh goodness, I know it's important if I did. I'm so close to both houses, aren't I? Both Felton's and Rupert's. Of course, it wasn't really Rupert's house, was it? It was Felton's, too. But it gets dreadfully confusing if I talk about Felton's house and Felton's house."

Beatrice was trying, and so far, succeeding at keeping her impatience in check. She said in a pleasant voice, "I think it *is* too confusing and we should just say Felton's house and Rupert's house."

Edith nodded complacently at this point having been established. "So this morning, I was inside all day long. I was doing laundry and baking." She looked eagerly at Wyatt and Beatrice for approval.

Wyatt gave her an encouraging smile and Beatrice gave her a tight one.

Edith continued, "So you're asking did I notice anything. Like a sound? Or a car? Or something like that?"

Wyatt said soothingly, "Anything unusual, really. Something that isn't usually there."

"Or maybe a person, cutting through yards on their way to Rupert's house," suggested Beatrice.

Edith considered this and then shook her head sadly as if dejected that she couldn't be helpful. "No. No, I didn't. But I was pretty focused on the laundry, I suppose. And then it was the baking. I had to decide what I wanted to bake, then I had to check to make sure I had all the ingredients. It was quite the busy morning."

Wyatt said, "That's all right, Edith. You didn't know you should be looking for anything unusual, after all."

Beatrice decided to try another tack and compliment Edith on the observation skills Beatrice still wasn't completely convinced Edith possessed. "Have you noticed anything unusual *lately*? I'm guessing you're around the house a good deal and you'd probably notice if something wasn't like it usually was. I'd imagine you were very good at noticing everyone's routine."

The ploy seemed to work and Edith puffed up proudly a little bit. "I am pretty good at that, as a matter of fact. You see, things happen at the same times, don't they? That's how I usually knew when was a good time to pop over and visit with Felton. I could see her lights turn on in her house in the morning and knew she was up. Then she'd be out in her garden about an hour later and I'd run by to say good morning. She was very routine-driven and would turn in at the same time every night, too. Of course, I didn't do the same thing with Rupert." She blushed at the thought. "I wouldn't pop by and visit him of course."

Beatrice attempted to get Edith back on course again. "So lately. In the days around both Felton's and Rupert's deaths, did you notice anything that struck you as a little different?"

Edith slowly nodded. "I suppose I did. I mean, it's not *that* different, but it wasn't the usual schedule. It's just Devlin, the yard man. He seemed like he's been hanging around a lot."

Beatrice raised her eyebrows. "Hanging around? Or doing yard work?"

Edith tilted her head to think this over. Then she said decidedly, "Hanging around. Just sitting in his truck and not doing any yard work. At the time, I thought maybe he was sitting in there and having a sandwich or something before he started working. But then he didn't work, he just drove on after a little while." She flushed. "Oh, I do feel bad about saying anything about Devlin. He did do such a good job with Felton's yard. But you just don't know what it's like for me right now. I've been *so* worried about my personal safety. I mean . . . a killer! And within sight of my house! I haven't been able to sleep or eat. It's been just awful."

Beatrice asked, "Do you think he could do something like that?"

Edith tearfully shook her head. "No, not really. I mean, who could? I feel like *no one* I know could have done it. Wasn't there a robbery, too? Missing pieces of jewelry? Maybe it was a total stranger who was trying to steal things from Felton."

Wyatt said gently, "It's hard to think that people are capable of this, isn't it?"

Edith nodded vigorously at him.

Beatrice said, "Unfortunately, that motive really won't work for Rupert, though, would it?"

Edith deflated in her chair, looking sadly at the empty plates of cookies. "No, I suppose not. No one would think Rupert had money. He lived in that little house that hardly had a stick of furniture in it."

"Have you noticed *Rupert* acting unusually?" asked Beatrice. "It seems like you had a good idea of your neighbors' routines. Was Rupert doing anything differently?"

Edith thought about this. "Well, I guess he was. Although, you know Rupert wasn't as structured as Felton was. That's funny, isn't it? You always think kids are going to be like their parents."

Wyatt said, "Maybe he was usually more structured but just hadn't developed one yet in a new town and a new house?"

This answer seemed to satisfy Edith and she gave a bob of her white head. "That could be true, yes. He seemed to keep kind of crazy hours. Sometimes Coco would wake me up in the middle of the night." She gave Coco, who was bathing herself in a sunbeam, a fond look. "She pounces on my feet under the sheets sometimes as if she thinks they're mice. Anyway, that's usually when I realize I need a cup of water or . . . the powder room." She flushed a little with a sideways apologetic glance at Wyatt for the indelicacy. "A couple of times when I've been up, I've noticed all the lights are on at Rupert's house."

"Did he have any visitors there? Or was he just staying up really late? I'd gotten the impression that he really didn't know anyone in town and had been keeping to himself," said Beatrice.

"I did look in his driveway, but there weren't any other cars there. It sort of sounded like a party, though. I could hear music playing." Edith frowned.

"Maybe that's how he tried to relax at night, listening to music?" asked Wyatt.

Edith seemed doubtful at this. "I suppose so. Except the music wasn't very relaxing-sounding. It was more like rock music. And it must have been pretty loud for me to be able to hear it over here, even with my hearing not as good as it used to be."

Beatrice said, "I know you and Felton were very close. I was wondering if you could answer a question for me."

Edith beamed at the mention of her closeness with Felton. "Of course I will. I mean, if I can."

"It's just that I've been speaking with a few people around town lately. You know how small towns are . . . people do like to talk about things that are happening."

"And they've been talking about Felton." Edith considered this. "You know, in some ways, I think Felton would like that. What are they saying?"

Beatrice hesitated. She didn't want to tell Edith that Lucius had questioned Felton's stories and the value of her ring. Instead of calling out names, she tried to make it general. "Well, some are saying that Felton was not in a very good financial situation. And that the jewelry she had was actually not valuable at all, but well-designed costume jewelry. I was just wondering if you knew anything about that at all. If Felton ever said anything to you." Beatrice watched with alarm as Edith's face grew hot with a red flush and she started getting as agitated as she'd been when they'd first arrived at her house.

Edith spat out, "But why would people say that when it wasn't true! Felton was from a fine family. She was a *blueblood*. She had plenty of money and nice jewelry."

Beatrice quickly added, "Maybe they're just jealous, that's all."

"Everything's okay, Edith," said Wyatt soothingly. He gave Beatrice a worried look.

"I'm sorry I brought it up," said Beatrice. "Of course you're right. Like I said, people just like to talk." This seemed to calm Edith down again. She took a big sip of water.

Beatrice decided to move carefully back to the previous subject before the catastrophic one. "So, going back to Rupert. We were trying to think about people he might have been connected with in town. But you haven't seen him with anyone else in town?"

Edith blinked a few times. "Oh! You know what, I *did* see him talking to someone recently. It made me wonder if maybe he'd found a friend. But it was the most unusual coincidence. Isn't it funny when coincidences happen? It's almost like déjà vu."

"Who was it?" asked Beatrice, once again trying to tamp down her impatience.

"Why, it was Rowesa Fant! Isn't that so funny? I'd just seen her with Felton right before poor Felton passed. I swear I never used to see Rowesa and now she's popping up everywhere!"

Chapter Thirteen

"Rupert and Rowesa were having a conversation?" asked Beatrice, trying to keep Edith focused.

"That's right." Edith frowned. "Although I'm not sure it was the friendliest conversation. At first, I wondered if maybe Rupert was making a friend. You know, Rowesa being single and Rupert being single. But then I could see that they didn't seem to be friendly at all."

"Were they arguing?" asked Beatrice.

"Yes, I think they were. Rowesa's hands were on her hips." Edith demonstrated. "And Rupert seemed angry and was looking around him like people might be listening in."

"Where were they?" asked Beatrice.

"Oh, goodness. I suppose I saw them at the grocery store. Yes, that's right, at Bub's. For half a second I thought I'd go over and talk to Rupert when I first saw him, but then I realized he was having this very intense discussion and decided not to," said Edith.

"Speak to him?" asked Beatrice.

"Yes. And now I feel just awful because I never got to, did I? I mean, after Felton died, I meant to go over to Rupert's house and bring some food of some sort. A casserole or something. That would have been the right thing to *do*." Edith looked disgusted with herself at the lapse. "But I never ended up going by his house. Actually, I should have gone by his house to bring him food when he first *arrived* at the house, too. After all, we were new neighbors."

Wyatt said, "But you haven't been in the right frame of mind yourself, have you?"

Edith gave him a startled look. "In what way?"

"Only that you haven't been sleeping or eating . . . isn't that what you were telling us?" asked Wyatt.

Edith nodded. "That's right. But that shouldn't excuse me from being decent and taking Rupert food and telling him how sorry I was about his mother's death. But I never went over there. I never did go to his house. And now it's too late for me to tell him."

Wyatt said, "You had no idea Rupert was going to die. Why would you?"

This seemed to cheer Edith up a little. "Oh, I'm *so* glad you came by. I do feel so much better now."

They visited a few more minutes while Edith briskly cleaned up their glasses and plates and then Wyatt and Beatrice set out back to their car. Beatrice heard Edith immediately lock the door behind them, still with an eye to security.

They walked the short distance back to their car, still outside Rupert's house. It looked like things were starting to settle down a bit there. Ramsay raised a hand in a wave as they drove away.

Wyatt said, "You know, it doesn't really get any easier."

"What doesn't?" Beatrice turned to look at him.

"The death of people you know. I've been a minister most of my life and have experienced death with families and it just doesn't seem to feel any more routine." Wyatt's eyes were tired as he looked out the windshield.

"Well, this one was slightly different, though, wasn't it? This wasn't a member of the congregation who's been sick for a long while and then passes away with all his family members gathered around. This was a middle-aged man with his life still ahead of him who had his life abruptly taken from him. It just feels wrong."

"You're right." He paused and gave Beatrice a quick glance. "What did you make of Edith's mention of Rowesa and Rupert?"

"And their 'unfriendly conversation', as Edith put it? Well, the first thing that came into my head is that we know Rupert was hurting for money," said Beatrice.

Wyatt nodded.

"And he had access to Felton's house and had likely just been in there to assess what would need to be done with her belongings and estate. Maybe he ran across some notes Felton had taken about Rowesa, or a diary of Felton's of some kind. Maybe Felton herself had even mentioned something to her son about it. I could picture her scolding him or warning him not to try Rowesa's methods for making money."

Wyatt pulled the car into their driveway. "So you're thinking Rupert, very short on cash, tried stepping into his mother's shoes to blackmail Rowesa."

"I think it's very likely, don't you?"

Wyatt said, "But it wouldn't have worked, would it? It didn't even work the first time because Rowesa decided not to pay up—or she *couldn't* pay up. And now Rowesa has confessed everything. There would be no reason for her to pay anything."

"No. But Rupert wouldn't know that. He wasn't in the loop at all. Maybe he thought it was something he could get away with."

They got out of the car. Beatrice smiled at Noo-noo in the front window, her foxy face grinning at them. It was so nice to have the little furry girl excited at seeing them come home.

Wyatt said, "But why would Rowesa have killed Rupert?"

Beatrice followed him inside and stooped to give Noo-noo a cuddle. "She wouldn't have. It simply doesn't make sense. I can't see that she had anything to do with that. But I do think Rupert approached Rowesa and tried to blackmail her. And, if he tried his hand at that, maybe he tried his hand at blackmailing Felton's killer." She sighed. "Plus, I have the annoying feeling that I learned something important but I can't figure out what it is."

Beatrice's phone pinged and she saw Chrissy Jo had sent her the pictures of her aunt's rug and decoys. She quickly forwarded them to her appraiser friends while it was still on her mind. Then Beatrice looked at her watch. "Almost time for Meadow to hand Will off. What are your plans for the rest of the day? Want to hang out with us or do you have things you need to do?"

Wyatt checked his calendar on his phone "It looks like Edgenora has scheduled me for a couple of pastoral visits this afternoon. I'll be at the hospital and at the church. And while I'm at the church office, I should probably knock out some of the paperwork I've got. Can you give Will a big hug for me?"

"That will be an easy assignment," said Beatrice with a chuckle.

Meadow wasn't exactly right on time for the baby handoff, which didn't surprise Beatrice since this very scenario had happened before on numerous occasions. Beatrice wasn't sure if Meadow simply lost track of time or whether she purposefully made her visits with Will last as long as humanly possible. She finally appeared at Beatrice's door with Will in his stroller and reluctantly handed over the baby and a bunch of baby equipment.

She handed off a bunch of tips, too. "When he has his diaper changed, he really likes if you sing *Row, Row, Row Your Boat*. It totally distracts him and makes him laugh."

Beatrice said grimly, "If I sing to him, he'll *really* laugh. Or, worse, cry."

Meadow added, "And when he goes down for naps, he loves if you wind up his little turtle pillow. It plays *Twinkle, Twinkle Little Star*."

Beatrice was feeling alarmed. "I don't have to sing that as well, do I?"

"Goodness no! No, just wind up the pillow and that's all you need to do. It's just very soft and sweet and helps him to settle down and fall asleep. Let's see. Oh! When you're playing with him, try playing 'where's Will?'"

"Now that one I think I might be able to handle. Peek-a-boo, right?"

"Exactly. Unfortunately, he slept most of the time at my house." Meadow looked dejected. "I'm not sure if he'll really be napping here at all."

Beatrice said wryly, "Oh, we'll have plenty of things going on here to wear him out. Noo-noo needs a walk, so we can go on a stroller ride. And Miss Sissy was planning on coming over to hold Will, apparently. Which reminds me that Savannah said she was going to come over and bring her cat. It's going to be a zoo."

As if on cue, the doorbell rang. Then it rang again. Then, impatiently at the two-second delay, again.

Beatrice rolled her eyes. "There she is now. Miss Sissy must have had binoculars out and staked out the house."

She opened the door and sure enough, there was Miss Sissy. Today she looked much better put-together than she had the day before. Her wiry gray hair was mostly shoved into the messy bun and she wore a floral long dress and, rather oddly, an apron. She only had eyes for Will and looked greedily at the baby Beatrice held. Miss Sissy reached out her bony arms for the child.

Meadow gasped with alarm. "Heavens, no! No, Miss Sissy! You might drop him."

Miss Sissy narrowed her eyes and gritted her teeth at Meadow, who quickly relented. "Um, why don't you sit down on the sofa here and Beatrice can hand him to you."

Miss Sissy trotted over to the sofa and held out her arms again. Beatrice carefully lay Will in them and the baby looked up curiously at the old woman.

Meadow muttered under her breath, "Well, good luck with all that."

"Miss Sissy's very strong, you know. I don't think she'd have any trouble holding Will."

Meadow nodded. "She's strong, all right. Strong-willed, too. You'll be babysitting *two* of them. And I hope you have lots of food in your house."

Usually Miss Sissy *did* eat Beatrice out of house and home when she visited. "I have the feeling this time she might be too distracted to eat as much as she usually does." Beatrice added. "By the way, how was Piper when you saw her this morning?"

Meadow blinked. "Piper? Oh, she was fine, I think. Why? *Isn't* she fine?"

Beatrice hid a smile. "Of course she's fine. She's the happiest she's ever been in her life, right now. Healthy, cute little boy and a husband she loves. Family who cares about her. I was just thinking she was looking a little slim lately."

Meadow's brow wrinkled. "Come to think of it, she *has* been looking a little thin, hasn't she? Especially for someone who had a baby not long ago."

Beatrice said, "That's probably just a side effect of not having a lot of sleep, getting plenty of exercise with Will, and not really having time to cook. But there's nothing we can do about any of that."

She waited for Meadow to assess this statement.

"By golly, there *is* something we can do about it! Or that *I* can do about it, anyway. You know how much I love to cook. I'll just start making extra servings and bringing Piper and Ash the extras. Besides, it will give me another chance to peek in on Will while I'm there." She hastily pulled her pocketbook out of Will's stroller and fumbled within its cavernous depths until she took out a pencil and a small notepad. "Okay, what are some of her favorite dishes?"

"Piper likes everything," said Beatrice with a shrug.

"Oh, come on, there's got to be something she *really* likes."

"Meadow, she'll be so delighted to have some good home cooking that she'll gobble up anything you bring by. You know she loves your food," said Beatrice.

"That's true, actually," said Meadow thoughtfully, tapping the pencil against her mouth. "Well, maybe I'll just do a rendition of Meadow's Greatest Hits. A lot of them are Ash's favorites and that will make it easy."

Miss Sissy growled something from the direction of the sofa and Meadow looked at her in alarm. "Something wrong, Miss Sissy? Need help with the baby?"

Miss Sissy scowled at her. "I said 'bring food today.'"

Apparently, Miss Sissy was still planning on being hungry, despite her focus on little Will.

Meadow looked at her doubtfully. "Well, I suppose I could. But I'll already be cooking quite a bit for us and for Piper and Ash."

Beatrice looked curiously at the wiry old woman. "Miss Sissy, what *do* you usually eat when you're at home?"

"Greens," she said shortly.

Meadow frowned at her. "Greens? What, like collard greens?"

Miss Sissy lifted an arthritic hand and started enumerating them. "Collard greens. Mustard greens. Turnip greens. Spinach. Cabbage."

"She'll live forever," murmured Beatrice.

Miss Sissy continued, although she was running out of fingers. "Broccoli."

"Is broccoli considered a green?" Meadow tilted her head and considered this.

"It's green," hissed Miss Sissy.

"Can't argue with her there," said Beatrice.

Meadow was still thinking about this. "And that's *all* you eat?"

Miss Sissy said, "And bananas."

"I'm not sure this all qualifies as a complete diet," said Meadow, frowning. "I'll have to refer to the food pyramid."

"Meadow, she's eating the healthiest foods out there. She'll outlive us all."

"Yes, but I think you're supposed to eat other things! Won't she end up with scurvy or rickets or something like that? I seem to recall those diseases from my elementary school health textbook." Meadow put her hands on her hips.

Beatrice asked, "Miss Sissy, how long have you been eating these foods? I mean, solely eating them?"

Miss Sissy pursed her lips in thought. She shrugged a thin shoulder. "Thirty years?"

"Thirty years!" exclaimed Meadow. "Holy cow!"

"No wonder she's gorging on junk food whenever she's out and about," said Beatrice.

Meadow said, "Well, I think I'm going to have to add you to my list of people who need a meal. But I won't bring you something *every* day, Miss Sissy. How about twice a week?"

Miss Sissy bobbed her head and looked pleased. Then, conversation apparently over, she refocused her attention on Will who was cooing at her.

Meadow said in her stage whisper that was a lot louder than she thought it was, "Do you suppose it's an economic thing with her? She's eating greens because they're cheaper?"

"But they're *not* cheaper. Healthy food is a lot more expensive than junk food. If it was a matter of money, she'd be eating French fries from fast food places all day." Beatrice called out to Miss Sissy, "Do you *like* greens? Or are you eating them for other reasons?"

Miss Sissy looked at her through narrowed eyes, annoyed at the interruption. "Like them fine. And they're easy to cook."

"There you are," said Beatrice to Meadow with a shrug.

Meadow said, "Okay. Well, to each his own. I'd better run . . . I need to figure out a menu for the week and run to the store." She hurried over to give Will a goodbye cuddle as Miss Sissy snarled at her. "See you later, Beatrice."

Chapter Fourteen

Miss Sissy decided to sing a few songs to Will, which he drank in with fascination, although Miss Sissy wasn't exactly a chanteuse and she made up most of the lyrics she'd forgotten. Beatrice strongly suspected one of them was a sea shanty. While the old woman was occupied, Beatrice left a message on Piper's phone to let her know Meadow was planning on fixing Piper's nonexistent food problem. Ramsay should be very pleased to have Meadow cooking supper once again.

The doorbell rang and Noo-noo gave an excited yelp, which made Will jump and Miss Sissy scowl.

Beatrice peered out and saw Savannah there with her little gray cat, Smoke. Smoke was wearing a red bow tie. Beatrice looked down at Noo-noo. "Can you be a good girl?"

Fortunately, Noo-noo was fond of cats. She'd gotten along well with Posy's Patchwork Cottage feline Maisie.

Beatrice stuck her head out. "Hi Savannah! Would you like me to put Noo-noo in the back bedroom, or do you think Smoke will be okay with her around?"

Savannah said, "Oh, Smoke loves dogs and Noo-noo is always really good. Leave her out."

Beatrice opened the door and asked Noo-noo to sit. Noo-noo sat perfectly still with an expression on her face that said 'please praise me.' So Savannah and Beatrice proceeded to do exactly that. Savannah carefully let Smoke say hello to the little corgi while Noo-noo was sitting like a statue and Smoke bumped his head against Noo-noo's as the corgi grinned at him.

"That's a very laid-back cat," said Beatrice.

Savannah nodded proudly. "Just like Maisie is. Maybe there's something in the Dappled Hills water."

Beatrice looked curiously out the door. "How did you get Smoke here? You were on your bicycle." Savannah and her sister might possibly be the fittest people in town since neither drove, but biked everywhere. Well, the fittest people aside from the greens-eating Miss Sissy.

"Georgia found this device online—look again," said Savannah, grinning at Beatrice.

Beatrice did and saw that there was a different sort of basket on the front of Savannah's street bike. She was accustomed to seeing one at the front, but this was different.

Savannah eagerly explained. "So there's a platform that attaches to the bike frame and a removable pet carrier attaches to it."

"Amazing. What on earth will they come up with next?"

Savannah added, "And it doesn't attach to the handlebars at all, so I'm free to steer. It's perfect. I can take Smoke everywhere."

"It's a good thing he's such a social cat," said Beatrice dryly.

Miss Sissy eyeing Savannah suspiciously from the sofa. Savannah walked over. "Don't worry, Miss Sissy, I won't take Will from you."

Miss Sissy still leveled Savannah with a stern look, but softened when she saw Smoke. The old woman was definitely a sucker for small, cuddly creatures of all sorts and she loved Smoke. She was co-owner, with Posy, of Maisie, the shop cat.

Will's eyes grew big and round when he spotted Smoke. Savannah sat down next to Miss Sissy and Will and kept Smoke on her lap. "See the sweet kitty?" she asked Will.

Will gave a chuckling gurgle and reached out to touch Smoke. Savannah gently held his hand. "See how to be gentle?" she asked, carefully directing his pudgy small hand to stroke Smoke.

Miss Sissy beamed at Will, Smoke, and even Savannah.

This went on for some time until Will's eyes started to grow heavy. Beatrice glanced at the clock.

"It's time for the baby's nap," she announced.

Miss Sissy glared at her.

"Would you like to put him in his crib? I've endured all kinds of instructions from Meadow on how to do it," said Beatrice with a chuckle. "I have a portable crib in the bedroom."

Miss Sissy didn't budge.

Beatrice sighed. "Or, I suppose, you could hold Will while he naps. I only hope he's not spoiled for life by that."

Miss Sissy sniffed and bobbed her head in satisfaction as if to say that she figured she'd win that fight.

Savannah followed Beatrice over to the dining area and sat with her so they could chat without waking Will. She set Smoke on the floor and he immediately trotted over to Noo-noo and curled up next to her. He gave himself a very short bath and then fell right to sleep, as did the little corgi.

With all the sleeping creatures, Beatrice was starting to feel a little like a nap, herself. She glanced over at Miss Sissy. Usually, the old woman was the first to fall asleep in almost any situation, snoring loudly. If she fell asleep on the sofa, Beatrice planned to spirit Will away and lay him in his portable crib. But this time, Miss Sissy looked very alert, still smiling benevolently down at the baby.

"How is everything going?" asked Savannah. She gave Beatrice an assessing look. "I heard about Rupert Billows. That's so odd that both members of that family are gone."

Beatrice nodded. "It's odd, for sure. And, of course, Wyatt and I had just visited with Rupert to hear his plans for his mother's service."

Savannah shook her head. "It's such a pity."

"Did you know Felton well? I thought I remembered you sometimes did things together," said Beatrice.

"We played chess sometimes," said Savannah.

Beatrice blinked at her. "I didn't realize you were a chess player." But now that she'd heard it, she couldn't see a game that would be more perfect for Savannah to play. Savannah was a very analytical person; the type of person who enjoyed math problems and geometric-styled quilts. Chess would be right up her alley, of course.

Savannah said, "When I can find someone to play with me, I love it. I play it on the computer a lot, but it's not the same as playing with another person. But even though Felton and I would play with each other, I didn't really feel like I knew her well."

Beatrice raised her eyebrows. "That's funny. I thought Felton loved to talk about herself." She made a face. "That sounds awful. I didn't really mean it that way."

"Don't worry, I know exactly what you're talking about. But besides all that, she didn't talk much about personal things. I never heard her talk about her son, for one. Except when he moved here and then she fussed about him and how he'd messed his business up and had to move back home. She talked about her family and her jewelry and that was about it. And that was just smoke and mirrors," added Savannah briskly.

"Smoke and mirrors?"

"I thought it was all fake. She talked about it too much for it to be real. And her stories got more and more fantastic the longer she told them." Savannah added, "You know I don't make a ton of money, but working as a CPA, I see people who *do* make a lot of money. They retire here and most of them never talk about all the money and the fancy things they have. Plus, sometimes I'd be playing chess with Felton at her house and the yard guy would ask to be paid and she'd say she didn't have any more checks or didn't have cash."

"Which made you think she didn't have much money, either."

"Exactly. The only person who looked like she believed her stories was Edith." Savannah shrugged. "And maybe she was starting to disbelieve them, herself, toward the end."

"What makes you think that?"

Savannah said, "She always used to talk about Felton in a really dreamy way. If Felton wasn't around to tell her stories, Edith would tell them for her. But a couple of weeks ago, she started getting really defensive when she talked about Felton. Like she was forcing herself to defend her and her stories when people in town talked about her. She was behaving differently, so I figured maybe she was finally putting two and two together. Of course, I'd never have said anything to make Edith look at Felton differently."

"That was kind of you not to say anything," said Beatrice.

Savannah shrugged. "I didn't really *know* those things. I just guessed."

Beatrice looked over at Will again. Miss Sissy was still looking very alert and awake as she continued her vigil over Will's sleeping form. Noo-noo had decided to trot over and sit right on Miss Sissy's feet. In a hushed voice, she told Savannah about Miss Sissy's daily diet. Savannah chuckled. In reality, though, Savannah herself frequently didn't eat all that well, although she was trying to do a better job lately.

Beatrice sighed. "I'm not sure what I'm going to do with Miss Sissy for the rest of the afternoon. Will might want to do something else after he's woken up and had a bottle. I have the feeling she won't want to put him down."

Savannah said, "You should take him on a stroller ride."

"And Miss Sissy?" asked Beatrice dryly.

"She can come along, too. Maybe you can go to June Bug's and Miss Sissy can have a snack." Savannah shuddered. "She clearly needs to eat something other than greens. Anyway, June Bug has someone new helping her out over there, so she probably has more time to visit. She probably wants to see Will. *Everybody* wants to see Will."

"Who's helping her out? Anyone we know?" asked Beatrice.

"You probably know her from church. Rowesa Fant."

Beatrice's eyebrows shot up. "Rowesa is helping June Bug?"

Savannah frowned at her reaction. "Well, sure. That's okay, isn't it? June Bug has really flexible hours so Rowesa figured she could fit in some work in-between running errands for the older lady she works for."

"Of course," said Beatrice. "I guess I just thought she already had a job, that's all." Beatrice couldn't help but wonder if June Bug had known all the facts before hiring Rowesa. But she wasn't sure it was something she should mention.

Savannah looked at the large watch she always kept half an eye on. "Smoke and I should be heading out. I need to feed him and start in on some paperwork."

Beatrice said, "And I'm going to take a picture of Smoke on the front of your bike. I want to see that."

Savannah said proudly, "He loves it! He's an amazing cat."

"He definitely is. Thanks for introducing him to Will. You could tell he was having fun."

Savannah's eyes softened. "His little face is very expressive." She glanced over at the still-fierce Miss Sissy. "I'd go over and say bye except, well, he's asleep and Miss Sissy is being scary."

"I think Will is going to understand," said Beatrice with a chuckle.

She watched as Savannah scooped up Smoke and the small gray cat happily climbed into the carrier on Savannah's bike as Savannah held it steady.

Beatrice took out her phone and snapped a picture of Smoke looking curiously out of the carrier at the world as Savannah got on the bike and posed with a smile.

"Thanks for coming by," said Beatrice as Savannah and Smoke set off down the street.

Will actually did seem to be taking a very sound nap, despite Beatrice not employing any of Meadow's prescribed actions to make it happen. Miss Sissy remained alert and Beatrice did some housework while Will continued snoozing.

Then she remembered Ramsay's short stories and pulled them out, curiously. She'd read Ramsay's poetry before and thought it was technically very good, if a little dry. She picked up the first story and read it. Then she read another and another. His short stories weren't dry at all, but rather flights of fancy and all very different from each other. One of them was set in outer space and focused on an exchange between two astronauts. Another was a gentle story of kids fishing on a warm summer day. Still another was set around the protagonist's strange dream and growing inability to separate reality from his dream world. She shook her head and thought again that Ramsay's creativity was wasted at the police station.

Finally, Will stirred a little and woke up, blinking at Miss Sissy as if trying to remember where he was and who this old woman was. She beamed down at him and he stuck a chubby finger in his mouth as he kept staring at her.

"I think it's time for Will to be changed and have a bottle," said Beatrice. She wondered if she might get out of diaper duty since Miss Sissy had been so determined to take over every aspect of babysitting.

Miss Sissy, however, didn't seem quite as interested in diaper changing. "I'll give him the bottle," she growled. She got up to help herself to a large snack while Beatrice got the changing pad, wipes, and diaper out of the diaper bag.

After Miss Sissy had fed Will, Beatrice said, "Let's give him a change of scenery, Miss Sissy."

Miss Sissy greeted this proclamation suspiciously.

"He's been in the house for a while and could probably use some fresh air. *I* could use some fresh air. Let's go on a stroller ride."

Miss Sissy scowled at this.

"We can visit June Bug. And then maybe stop by and see Posy before Piper picks up Will."

Miss Sissy reluctantly capitulated after asking, "And eat at June Bug's?"

It was amazing to Beatrice that Miss Sissy could possibly want another bite of food after the tremendous amount she'd swiftly consumed during the diaper change. But she nodded. "If you want to. Is there something over there you especially like?"

"Cupcakes," said Miss Sissy, grinning greedily at the idea.

So they set out for downtown. Although they were walking at a sedate pace on the sidewalk, Miss Sissy snarled at every car that passed by, as if convinced they meant to suddenly swerve off the road and smash into them. Which was ironic, because, since Felton's untimely demise, the only remaining citizen of Dappled Hills fond of driving on sidewalks was Miss Sissy, herself.

June Bug's shop was quiet when they got there and June Bug and Rowesa both glanced up and smiled when they opened the door.

"Cupcakes," said Miss Sissy immediately.

June Bug, apparently familiar with Miss Sissy's usual order, quickly put together a small plate. "Peanut butter and chocolate, red velvet, and banana caramel," she said cheerfully as she set it in front of the old woman.

Miss Sissy greedily attacked the peanut butter and chocolate while Rowesa watched in amazement as the wiry old woman quickly devoured it.

Beatrice said to June Bug, "Looks like you've got a great new helper, here."

June Bug beamed. "A hard worker!" she said. June Bug had hired on several part-time workers to help her manage the busy shop at different times.

There was a toot of a horn outside and June Bug looked out to see a delivery truck edging around to the back of the store.

"Excuse me," she said with a shy smile as she set out to check the deliveries off her inventory list.

The shop was empty and Beatrice pushed a chair slightly out. "Sit with us?" she said to Rowesa.

Rowesa said, "Just for a minute, thanks." She paused. "I know you're good friends with June Bug and I just wanted to let you know I told her all about what happened. I didn't want to be hired under false pretenses."

This relieved Beatrice, although she was careful not to show it. "I'm sure you did. I know June Bug was glad to hire you — she always needs an extra set of hands here."

"The best thing was that she can use me for odd hours. I don't really have a set schedule working for Mrs. Bradwell, but June Bug is happy to have me here whenever I can help out. She's been so generous. And for extra money, I'm also going to be babysitting her niece when she needs help sometimes. Katie's a little love."

Beatrice nodded. "She is."

Rowesa's face suddenly darkened. "But I heard about Mrs. Billows's son, Rupert."

Beatrice said, "Word travels quickly here."

"Ramsay and a state policeman came here to ask me about it earlier, and that's how I found out."

Beatrice remembered Edith talking about Rowesa's and Rupert's "unfriendly" conversation. "Did you ever meet him?"

Rowesa nodded and swallowed hard. "I did. As a matter of fact, he approached me. He tried to blackmail me the way Mrs. Billows did."

Beatrice made a face. "I'm so sorry. How did he know about it?"

Miss Sissy finished off the last of her cupcakes. Will cooed at her and she grinned at him, reaching over to play peek-a-boo with the baby.

Rowesa shrugged helplessly. "I have no idea. Maybe she told him about it or maybe he found some notes in her papers in the house. But it didn't work, of course. I told him I'd already gone to the police and confessed everything. He didn't have any power over me."

"How did he react when you said that?"

Rowesa sighed. "He was so angry. And we were out in public, too. He'd caught up with me at the grocery store. I guess he'd thought he could get some money out of me. Not that I have anything to give. When I told him I wasn't going to give him a cent, he was furious."

"What was Ramsay's reaction when you told him about it?"

Rowesa said, "I couldn't really tell. I *think* he believed me. But I didn't have any alibi for Rupert's death because I was running around town doing errands for Mrs. Bradwell. As far as he's concerned, I could have popped by Rupert's house and killed him while I was out."

Beatrice said, "But surely he realizes there was no reason for you to have done such a thing."

"Exactly. There's no reason at all. The state policeman asked a question that made it sound like he thought maybe I had another conversation with Rupert at his house, got frustrated with him, and lashed out." Rowesa's face was clouded with worry.

"But why on earth would you have done that?"

Rowesa said slowly, "The policeman seemed to think maybe Rupert was talking about spreading the story all over town. That maybe I was worried about my reputation. That I'm not worried about going to jail anymore, but wouldn't want the whole town to know what I'd done. I mean, I do have to live here and he's right in a way—I wouldn't want people to talk about me or my daughter and look at us differently."

"And *did* Rupert threaten to gossip about you?"

Rowesa shook her head. "He was more focused on telling the police. But who knows? Maybe he would have come back later and threatened me with gossip. I promise I had nothing to do with his death."

She looked so alarmed by the idea that Beatrice reached out and patted her arm reassuringly. She asked, "While you've been driving around and running errands, have you happened to see anything unusual at Rupert's house?"

"Unusual?" asked Rowesa.

"I gather Rupert didn't have many visitors since he really didn't know anyone in Dappled Hills," said Beatrice.

Rowesa snorted. "And he apparently wasn't very good at making friends, either."

Beatrice gave her a wry smile. "His tactics were definitely suspect."

Rowesa considered the question. "Well, I wasn't paying a lot of attention until just very recently. And then I was looking out for him because I was trying to avoid him. But I did notice his yard guy was over there a couple of times. I thought that was kind of weird. It wasn't a big yard and it was so shady that I didn't think there was much grass to be mowed." She shrugged. "Other than that, I didn't see anything."

The bell on the door rang and she quickly said, "Better run. Good to see you."

The customer was Chrissy Jo who smiled when she saw Beatrice.

Beatrice waved at her and she came over. Miss Sissy gave Chrissy Jo a ferocious sideways look until she realized she was coming over to speak to Beatrice and not try to hold the baby.

Beatrice said, "Thanks for sending the photos over. I went ahead and forwarded them to my appraiser friends."

Chrissy Jo grinned at her. "Oh, I know you did. They both already got in contact with me. I sent them a few more pictures, zooming in on some spots they were asking about. And Beatrice, I can't thank you enough. The rug *and* the decoys are valuable and they are going to advise me on how best to auction them off. And I owe it all to you. Before you spoke to me, my plan was to stick everything in the car and take it off to Goodwill."

"I'm just happy I could help," said Beatrice. "And really glad they're worth something, too."

They chatted for a moment before Chrissy Jo's friend joined her and they set to ordering cake slices with June Bug.

Chapter Fifteen

Since Miss Sissy was already casting longing looks at the cupcake display again, Beatrice abruptly decided it was time for their little caravan to head on.

"Let's go," said Beatrice.

"Want to see June Bug," grumbled Miss Sissy.

"She's working on inventory." Beatrice was firm.

"Want to push the stroller." Miss Sissy appeared unwavering on this point.

"All right. But not too quickly; I know how you dash around sometimes. Let's visit Posy."

Miss Sissy led the way, although she tempered her usual trotting pace to a more sedate stroll this time. She continued hissing at drivers, this time shaking her fist in case they didn't get the idea that they mustn't be anywhere within twenty yards of the stroller.

The shop was bustling when they walked in. In fact, the entire Cut-Ups guild appeared to be inside. Posy gave them a quick wave and continued helping customers while her shop assistant checked people out at the register.

Miss Sissy was giving all the quilters warning looks between narrowed eyes to keep them away from Will's stroller. And the stroller, in fact, was taking up a good deal of room.

Beatrice said, "Let's get you settled in a chair with Will, Miss Sissy. I'll push the stroller out of the way."

"Sofa," the old woman said and gestured to the cushy sofa where Maisie the shop cat was already in residence.

Soon Miss Sissy and Will were on the sofa and Will was being charmed by the cat as the old woman looked on proudly.

There was actually no free spot for Beatrice to sit because the other chairs in the shop were taken up with quilters. She chatted with one of them, who was working on what looked to be a cheerful quilted bag in a deep pink and light green.

"That's a nice tote," said Beatrice.

The quilter smiled at her. "It's a friendship bag. I just used strips of cloth and pieced them together. It's an easy project. Then I'll give the bag to a quilting friend to help keep organized. If it's for Christmas or a birthday then sometimes I throw in fat quarters or charm packs."

Beatrice started feeling that familiar itch again—it was time to start a new project. She'd felt inspired at the guild meeting, but then had gotten busy again and hadn't started. She told herself that once she got back home she'd begin to do some work.

Her phone rang and she excused herself and stepped a few feet away.

"Hi, Mama," said Piper. "I've wrapped up early at the school today and I thought I'd run by and pick up Will. Are y'all at home?"

"Actually, we're at the Patchwork Cottage. Although good luck prying Will out of Miss Sissy's arms," said Beatrice dryly.

Piper chuckled. "I think Ash and I might be the only people she defers to when it comes to Will. Fingers crossed, anyway. Okay, I'll be right there."

A few minutes later, she walked in. A few of the Cut-Up guild members had trickled out, but there were still a lot of them shopping. Piper walked over to the sitting area and smiled at Miss Sissy who grudgingly smiled back, sensing her time was up. At least she could transfer her attention to Maisie.

"Want to see Will?" she asked Piper.

"If it's all right," said Piper. "Thanks for taking such good care of him today."

Piper leaned over and picked the baby up and his whole face lit up as he saw her. She crooned to him and gave him a cuddle and Will reached up to touch her face.

"How did everything go today?" asked Piper.

"With Will? Perfectly. He was such a good baby. He might be spoiled rotten after this morning, although I really hope not. Miss Sissy wouldn't relinquish him for anything, so he had his nap in her lap and not in a crib. But we had a nice stroller ride and went to June Bug's and here. Savannah came by with Smoke, and that was fun."

Piper creased her forehead. "But there was something else?"

"Well, nothing to do with Will. But this morning, when Wyatt and I were out earlier, we found out that Rupert Billows has died."

Piper's eyes grew huge. "No way."

"That's what we thought, too," said Beatrice.

Piper said slowly, "Was it natural causes, then, or . . . not?"

"I'm afraid not. He was murdered, like his mother was."

Piper shook her head. "What's going on here? Did you talk to Ramsay?"

"Only a little bit. He sounded like he had a few leads, but there haven't been any arrests yet."

Posy joined them as the shop finally emptied out. "Sorry about that! The Cut-Ups have a service project and they all came at the same time." She grew serious at Piper and Beatrice's solemn faces.

Beatrice quickly filled her in, keeping the account as undramatic as possible.

Posy's eyes still filled with tears. "That whole family is gone! It's just awful. Does Ramsay have any ideas?"

Beatrice said soothingly, "He's on it. I think he does have some leads." She thought back to the ring in Devlin's truck. At least Lucius was off the hook for this crime, considering he was in the local jail at the time. It reminded her that she and Wyatt had promised to visit him again.

Piper said, "Well, I guess I'd better take this little guy home." She looked over at the sofa, as if expecting a protest from Miss Sissy and grinned. "Looks like he managed to wear everyone out."

Miss Sissy, now off-duty since she was no longer responsible for holding Will, had fallen into a deep sleep and was snoring loudly.

Posy gave Will a goodbye cuddle, but Beatrice could see that she still seemed worried. She said, "I need to head off too, but I wanted to see some of your new fabrics before I go. I'm going to do the quick and easy project to get back into quilting again, but I have the feeling that seeing a new fabric for my next project might give me some inspiration, too."

Posy brightened and happily took Beatrice on a tour of the newest fabrics. Although it had mostly been a ruse to get Posy's mind off Rupert's death, Beatrice felt herself be drawn in as she saw all the colorful patterns and prints. She finally decided on a print with blue, green, and orange medallions.

Beatrice checked out and said, "Should I take Miss Sissy back home?"

"Oh, don't wake her up. She can rest here for a while and then hang out with Maisie. I'll take her home when it's time to lock up," said Posy.

Beatrice's phone rang and she excused herself and picked up. It was a woman from the church Chancel Guild. They needed a different sort of vase from a particular church closet but the woman who had the key was out of town. They'd tried calling Wyatt, but he was visiting church members at the hospital in Lenoir.

Beatrice gave Posy a quick hug and took off for home. She grabbed the key, gave Noo-noo a pat, then headed off to the church.

While she was there, she decided to check in with Edgenora in the church office. It occurred to her that Edgenora really should have a set of keys to everything, too. She'd run it by Wyatt, but couldn't see a reason why she shouldn't have them to keep in a locked drawer in the office.

When she arrived at the office, she stopped short. Ramsay was there, looking grim. Haskell was there, looking unrepentant.

And his mother Betty was there, looking very stressed out. Edgenora gave Beatrice a look.

"Should I come back another time?" asked Beatrice.

Ramsay looked at Betty and Betty quickly said, "Stay, Beatrice, if you don't mind."

Edgenora, mindful of their privacy, closed the glass window that partitioned off the reception part of the office and started busily working on the computer.

Beatrice was used to Haskell being almost obsequious, but he wasn't today. His face was thunderous and he was looking up at Ramsay defiantly.

Ramsay sighed. "Like I was saying, son, I'm just asking some routine questions. I'm having to ask the same questions of everyone who was close to the victims."

"I'm not your son," growled Haskell.

Ramsay bobbed his head. "True. Look, all I want to do is get to the bottom of this."

Haskell said, "Yeah, but you said you're talking to people who were close to them. Maybe I was close to Mrs. Billows, but I never even met this other guy. I've never seen him in my life."

Ramsay looked over to Betty again and her face clouded over. In a gentle voice, she said, "But Haskell, you have. You've got to tell the truth."

He glowered at her. "So you're not taking my side anymore? Is that how this is working?"

Betty shook her head. "There aren't any sides. There's just the truth and lies. I'm not going to stand here and let you tell lies." She gave a short laugh. "Here in the church!"

"You don't even know if I met him or not." There was a jeering tone to Haskell's voice that was jarring to Beatrice. This was another side to him that she'd never seen before. He'd always been so deferential when he'd spoken around her before.

Betty said in a quiet voice, "But I do. You told me after Mrs. Billows died, he'd gotten in touch with you to give you some errands to run for him. Remember?"

Ramsay said, "You confirm that you were acquainted with Rupert Billows?"

Haskell looked at him stubbornly before finally rolling his eyes and muttering an assent. "But barely," he added.

Ramsay nodded. "Can you tell me where you were this morning?"

"What time?"

"How about *all* the times. Just a basic rundown of your morning." Ramsay took out his small notepad and stubby pencil.

"Well, I got a later start this morning, since it's the weekend. I was home until something like eleven," he said smoothly.

He gave Betty a quick, sideways warning look which made Beatrice think he was both lying and asking his mother to cover for him.

Betty's eyes filled with tears and she shook her head, sadly. "No, you weren't."

Haskell lifted his chin. "You were just busy in the back of the house. But I was there."

She shook her head again, this time with conviction. Beatrice gave her arm a squeeze and Betty gave her a grateful look in return.

"Mom!" he hissed at her, standing up from his chair.

Ramsay stood quickly, too. "Sit down and keep talking. Tell me where you *really* were."

Haskell said, "Why do you even care? I had nothing to do with this stuff. You're just wasting your time. Why aren't you looking at the yard guy? He's the one you should be talking to." He gave his mother a taunting look.

"The yard guy?" Ramsay tilted his head to one side.

Haskell shrugged. "Seems likely to me. Like I told you before, he was upset with Mrs. Billows about not getting his money. Maybe he decided to steal from her. You know—steal something he could sell. She could have caught him in the act and he could have killed her. Then, maybe, Mrs. Billows's son found out about it and he had to kill him to keep him quiet."

Ramsay said, "Are you sure *you* weren't the one upset with not being paid? That *you* didn't steal from her and got caught in the act and killed Rupert Billows to keep him quiet?"

"I'm sure," said Haskell sharply.

Ramsay said, "This isn't a game, Haskell. I need to know where you were this morning. You weren't at home."

"You seem to have it all figured out. Why don't you tell *me*," he said in a jeering voice.

Betty said in a pleading voice, "Answer him, Haskell. You didn't do this. I know you didn't. Ramsay's right—you can't play around with this or you're going to end up in jail."

"I'm not playing around. I'm just frustrated the cops aren't looking at Devlin and are wasting time talking to me."

Ramsay said calmly, "You seem to have a lot of animosity against him."

Haskell snorted. "I don't really know the guy, except that he's dating my mom." He gave Betty a withering look. "I didn't have anything to do with any of this, all right? I wasn't at home, but I went to meet up with a friend. And that's it."

"Did you go somewhere that we can verify?"

He flushed and shrugged. "I guess. Maybe. I don't know. We just went over to the diner. I'm not sure if anybody there would even remember me. It was pretty busy there."

Betty breathed a sigh of relief at this. "But what friend was it?"

"Someone you don't know."

Betty said, "It's just that your friends always sleep in on the weekends." Beatrice saw a grain of doubt enter her eyes.

"It's a new friend, Mom. Someone you don't know." There was a warning tone in his voice.

Ramsay poised his pencil over the pad. "I'm going to need the name of this friend. To help verify where you were and when."

Haskell was silent for a minute. Then he finally muttered something out.

"Could you repeat that, please?" asked Ramsay.

Betty leaned in to hear.

"Dawn Playford!" he flushed. "Satisfied?"

"Do you have contact information for her?" asked Ramsay.

Haskell pulled his phone out of his pocket, punched at it for a minute, then read out the number.

Ramsay nodded and closed his notebook. "Well, you should be grateful to this young woman. If it all pans out, she'll be your alibi."

"Can I go now?" his voice was a little desperate.

Betty stood up. "I'll take you back."

"No, I've got my bike, remember?"

"I can take you *and* the bike back," she said but he was already gone.

Chapter Sixteen

Ramsay said politely, "I should be making my way out now, too. Thanks for being here while I spoke to Haskell, Betty."

"I'm so sorry for his attitude. He's not usually like that, you know."

Ramsay said, "It's all fine, Betty. I was a parent of a teenager once myself, you know. I remember."

Beatrice couldn't imagine that Ash had ever been anything remotely like Haskell.

After Ramsay left, Betty apologized to Beatrice, too. "It was so good to have someone here for support. That was hard for me to listen to."

Beatrice gave her a reassuring smile. "But it ended up all right, didn't it? It sounds as if he's got at least one alibi."

Betty said, "Oh, I hope so. I really do. I've been praying about Haskell every night. He's become such a handful and I can't figure out why. He never used to be like this. And I don't always know where he is or who his friends are. They're mostly new friends."

Beatrice said, "Do you worry about these new friends of his? Do you think they're trouble?"

"That's the thing—I really don't know them. But I admit, I don't like the looks of the ones I've briefly met. They're a tough looking group of kids. I've tried to keep track of Haskell. I mean, he drives, of course, but we're sharing a car so it's not as if he can just go off all day long. But *they* drive, so they come and pick him up. Who knows where they go and what they do?"

Beatrice wondered if the new friends and the sudden change in Haskell might mean that they'd introduced him to drugs. But Betty was already so strung out by Ramsay's interview that she hesitated to say anything. She asked instead, "Are his grades still good? Consistent?"

Betty shook her head. "That's another thing. He always made really good grades. He was at the top of his class. And now he should really be pouring it on—taking hard classes and do-ing really well because he'll be applying to colleges before long. But now his grades are slipping and his teachers are calling me. Sometimes he's even skipping school and he never did that be-fore." She paused, flushing. "I just hope you ignore what he said about Devlin."

"How is that relationship going?" asked Beatrice gently.

Betty's flush deepened and she smiled. Haltingly, she said, "I don't think I realized it was anything more than a friendship at first. I'm at the church a lot, you know. Everyone here has been so good, so supportive."

Beatrice said, "From everything Wyatt tells me, you're prac-tically indispensable here. I don't know what we'd do without all your volunteering for different programs and service work."

Betty looked pleased. "Well, it's my way of paying back. I've gotten so much from the services and the congregation. It's my pleasure to help out here. Anyway, Devlin would see me from time to time while he was working for Mrs. Billows and I was there to pick up Haskell. Sometimes he needed the car to run errands for her, but sometimes she needed him to lift things in the house for her or bring things down from the attic or stuff like that. While I'd wait for him to wrap up, we'd talk a little bit."

Beatrice had a hard time envisioning this. In her experiences with Devlin, he'd proven to be rather taciturn and reluctant to open up. He must have been interested in Betty right off the bat.

"He'd ask what my plans were for the evening and I'd mention my Bible study group or women's circle. He seemed like he was interested in the different things going on at the church. I don't think he knew all the programs we have. So I got very enthusiastic and would tell him all about the different things and encourage him to come."

Beatrice nodded. "He'd seemed interested in the programs at the church when Wyatt and I spoke with him recently."

Edgenora came out from the office and looked at Beatrice and Betty questioningly.

Betty smiled at her and said, "I think everything's good. Haskell has an alibi."

Edgenora said, "That's wonderful, Betty."

Betty sighed. "He could have just saved us all a lot of trouble if he'd mentioned it right off the bat. Apparently, it's one of his new friends."

Edgenora nodded, but there was a concerned look in her eyes. She knew Haskell's newer friends usually weren't up to much good.

Betty read the look accurately. "Oh, this is a new friend who's a *girl*. I think he was trying to keep it under wraps, but I guess that's impossible with a murder investigation." She gave a somewhat hysterical laugh and then put her hand over her mouth.

Beatrice said, "The good news is he's in the clear." Beatrice crossed her fingers. She wondered if it were possible for Haskell to have had his deli breakfast *and* gone by Rupert's house. Or maybe even simply planted that ring in Devlin's truck.

Betty said, "Yes. Which makes me feel even worse. I thought he *might* have done it. I just hate that I was even thinking that. But he's been so different lately and I haven't been able to figure him out. It's almost like I don't even know him anymore. I just can't believe I thought he could possibly be involved in something like this."

Edgenora said, "You're just worried about him, that's all."

"And he's been really unhappy about my relationship with Devlin." She flushed again. "I'm not even sure exactly what kind of a relationship it is. I was just explaining to Beatrice that he started out really interested in the church and I was kind of a guide to all the programs."

Edgenora snorted and bobbed her head until her white hair bobbed along with it. "If he'd only wanted a guide to all the church programs, he'd have asked *me*."

"I think he's interested in more than just the church programs," agreed Beatrice.

Betty smiled. "I think so, too. But we're off to a pretty bad start, what with him being hauled off for questioning and Haskell trying to throw suspicion on him."

Beatrice said, "But there has to be more to it than just suspicion for Ramsay to arrest someone. There has to be proof. I'm sure he'll be found in the clear."

They all left just moments later, Betty headed out to defuse Haskell, and Edgenora to eat dinner with Savannah. Beatrice was going to head back home to start supper, but remembered Lucius. She texted Wyatt to ask if he was free to join her in a visit with him, but he replied that he was visiting at the retirement home. She headed out herself.

Lucius seemed grateful to see her again.

"Do you have any idea how things are going?" she asked.

"Well, it seems I'm in the clear for another, possibly connected murder. So I believe most of the trouble I'm facing isn't here in Dappled Hills, but in other cities." He paused. "Maybe you can fill me in, since I didn't get all the details."

Beatrice quickly did. "Did you ever meet Rupert Billows?"

"I did. I tried to be a good ambassador for Dappled Hills," he said with a reminiscent smile.

"What was your impression of him?"

"As a matter of fact, I saw him with his mother. They were both in her garden when I was walking by and I took it upon myself to introduce myself, although I have to admit they seemed to be in the middle of some sort of argument."

Beatrice nodded. "Apparently they had a kind of uneven relationship."

"I could see that. He seemed a little sketchy to me. Which was funny because I understood he'd had this completely legitimate business that he'd rapidly over-expanded. But once he'd fallen on hard times, it looked to me that he might be considering other, less-legitimate opportunities."

"What makes you think that?"

"Oh, I don't know. It's just a particular quality one criminal can see in another, I suppose." Lucius's voice was wry. "He may not have been good at it. Having a proclivity for breaking the law doesn't necessarily mean you have a talent for it. I'm guessing he ran up against the wrong person and that's why he's no longer with us."

Beatrice nodded. "Is there anyone else involved in this who you see some bad qualities in?"

Lucius said, "Well, as I've mentioned before, Haskell is a mess. He might not always appear that way and I think the world of his mother, but there it is."

"A mess?"

"Exactly. He's on drugs. I don't know how he really managed that with his mother on top of him as she is and in a small town like Dappled Hills, but he did," said Lucius. "You can see it in his eyes. In his behavior."

"I saw a bit of that behavior today," said Beatrice.

"Right. Not like usual sulky teen stuff, either."

Beatrice said, "Apparently, he has some new friends and visits Lenoir sometimes with them."

"Well, that could definitely be where he's going off-track. If I could speak with Betty, I'd tell her about it. But I won't have that opportunity."

Beatrice sighed. "I wish you could. You'd be a lot better at it than I would. I guess I could mention something, even though I don't have any proof at all. It was something I wondered about today when I saw how he was acting. But as a mother, I can't imagine hearing that the minister's wife thinks your child is on drugs."

Lucius shook his head. "You don't have to approach it that way. You can just say, 'as a friend, I'm worried about Haskell.' You already have her ear and she trusts you. Yes, she might be a little defensive at first, but maybe it will come as a relief in some ways—it may be an issue she can fix. She'll just need some professional help."

Beatrice nodded. She said thoughtfully, "I know you realized early that Felton's jewelry was fake and her stories, too. It was nice of you not to say anything to Felton about it. Those stories and the fake jewelry seemed to be very important to her."

"She must have had some very deep insecurities to have concocted such a backstory. But she got away with it."

"Did you mention to anyone at all that Felton's jewelry wasn't real?" asked Beatrice.

Lucius looked at her for a moment and sighed. "Only one person and only recently. I've felt badly about it, especially since I've had so much time to think. But one day I was walking out of the library and Edith was coming in. I asked Edith how she was doing, but all she could do was talk about how *Felton* was doing, as if she didn't have any life of her own."

Beatrice said, "I wonder if she really did. Maybe now she'll be able to come out from under Felton's shadow. So you told Edith?"

"I tried to soften the blow. I just tried to usher in some doubts to her mind. I did it to be kind, but now I'm wondering if it was kind. Felton was her whole world, after all. I don't know how anyone would react on hearing their whole world was something of a sham." Lucius's face was lined with regret.

"How did she take the news?"

Lucius shook his head. "Not well. She was very angry with me. Then she burst into tears and ran away."

"And she was the only one who knew they weren't real?"

Lucius said, "Well, she was the only one I told, anyway. I'm not sure if others in town had their doubts, but they didn't get their doubts from me."

Beatrice nodded and then said, "Wyatt and I are going to miss you, Lucius. I wish I could have brought you something to read, at least. I did call over here, but the deputy said I wasn't allowed to."

He smiled at her, though his eyes were tired. "Well, once I'm in my permanent location, which I suspect may be rather soon, I'll have access to a prison library. Sometimes even book clubs. And they're better than you'd think they might be."

Beatrice smiled back at him, but knew he was making light of his predicament for her benefit. He didn't want his friend to worry about him. She placed thoughts of prison overpopulation and violence firmly out of her head. The last thing she wanted was to make Lucius feel badly when he was being optimistic.

Lucius grew serious. "And now, I thank you very much for your visit and your and Wyatt's concern. But you need to go spend time with your sweet grandbaby and your family. I'll be just fine, don't you worry. It's time for me to pay my debt to society. Maybe you can both drop me a line sometime? I'll send my address when I have it."

Beatrice smiled at him and stood up to leave. "We'd love to."

As she left the lockup area and walked into the small police department's lobby, Ramsay was coming in with a couple of state police officers. He beamed at her.

"Seeing Lucius? I'm glad you had a visit in. There's transport arriving tomorrow to pick him up and take him to New York."

"Then I'm glad I made it too. I know he did some bad things, but part of me hopes he won't be in there too long," said Beatrice.

Ramsay shook his head. "I'm afraid it's probably not going to work out that way, considering the charges and the different states that are piping up with their own allegations of wrongdoing. But I do know Lucius has a good lawyer because he mentioned him to me. At least the lawyer will ensure he's in as good a situation as possible." He grinned at Beatrice. "Okay, change of topic here. But I need to thank you. You're a magician."

"Am I?"

"It sure seems so to me. I've just eaten high on the hog at home. And Meadow even packed a snack for me to eat later!" He patted his generous tummy in satisfaction. "Now tell me how you managed that. I was eating peanut butter sandwiches on stale bread before you got involved."

"A little bird might have told Meadow that Piper could use a little extra help in the kitchen. That she and Ash were overwhelmed with other stuff and neither of them had time to focus on planning and cooking healthy meals." Beatrice chuckled.

"Genius! And the bonus is that Piper and Ash are probably eating better, too."

Beatrice said, "They are. Piper and Ash were still cooking, but I think a lot of scrambled eggs were happening over there. This way, they get some variety and more time to just relax instead of trying to figure out what's happening for supper. Miss Sissy is, too, since she wrangled meals from Meadow twice a week." She paused and added in a low voice, "I couldn't help but notice that Devlin wasn't here. The last I saw, he was in your police cruiser."

"Yep. The ring thing didn't really pan out and he was released. Turns out the ring was wiped of fingerprints, which seems like an odd thing for Devlin to have done, if he'd been the one to put it in his truck. So we're still looking. Have you heard anything on your end?"

Beatrice shook her head. "Not really. Well, nothing concrete, anyway. People gossiping about other people, that sort of thing. You know the kind of stuff I usually hear about."

Ramsay nodded. "Got it. Sounds like what we're getting, too. Plus a lot of leads that just don't pan out. Well, if you hear anything, can you let me know? What are your plans for the rest of the day?"

"I'll definitely let you know. As far as plans go, I think I probably need to try to relax." Beatrice grimaced. "Although you know that's not usually what works out for me."

Ramsay chuckled. "Yeah, I know that. Going to take a stab at focusing on your book. What's the name of it again?"

"*The Sweetness at the Bottom of the Pie*."

"Oh, right, the mystery." He made a face. "Maybe I'll be in the mood for a mystery after this one wraps up. Right now, there's a little too much mystery going on."

"I know what you mean. As a matter of fact, I *don't* think I'll read. I'm going to try to do some quilting for once. That way I can fidget a little bit while I'm working on it." Beatrice snapped her fingers. "I've been meaning to tell you that I read your short stories."

Ramsay gave her a surprised grin, although there was a hint of anxiety in his eyes. "I can't believe you found the time to do that with everything you've got going on. I thought you'd get back to me in a couple of weeks."

"I sort of thought I would, too. Maybe it was curiosity that made me pick them up, but once I started reading them, I couldn't stop."

Ramsay, who'd been holding himself tightly, relaxed suddenly and looked relieved. "Oh, that's good to hear. Unless you couldn't stop reading them because it was like watching a train wreck."

She shook her head. "Not at all. They were great. And I loved the way they were all so different from each other. I thought there might be a common theme at least, but the themes were even original. I think you need to seriously consider submitting them to contests or a literary magazine."

Ramsay's face broken into a wide grin. "Really? You're not just saying that?"

Beatrice chuckled. "No way. Remember, my job was to curate art at a museum. I never told people what they wanted to hear."

"That's the best news I've heard in a long time." He ruminated on the stories for a few moments. "Hm. Maybe I should fish out the poetry, too."

Beatrice cleared her throat. "Remember how I said I never told people what they wanted to hear?"

"Uh-oh. So the poetry is a no?"

Beatrice said, "It's your poetry so you should do what you want to do. And art is very subjective."

"And . . . what else?" asked Ramsay.

"And, for me, it's technically good but it might be a little dry. Maybe you could do some revising and think about sending it out the next go-round?" She laughed wryly. "Or ignore me and go ahead and send it out. After all, what do I know about poetry?"

Ramsay said, "You read poetry and probably know a lot more about it than anybody else around here. I'll give it a little more work. But the short stories?"

"They're amazing," said Beatrice, meaning it.

One of the state policemen called to Ramsay. "Good luck with your reading," he said as he turned to join the others.

Back at home, Beatrice did get some work done. After feeding Noo-noo, she got out a bunch of her old fabrics to see which might work together for the strip quilt. She had a lot more fabric than she'd remembered—just bits and pieces from old projects. She picked out a few that color-coordinated well together and got to work.

About thirty minutes later, she'd definitely made headway, but was starting to get restless. Her brain kept returning to Felton's and Rupert's deaths and all the conversations she'd had with the people who were involved with their lives.

Finally, in frustration, she stood up. Noo-noo stood up too, looking quizzically at her.

"I need to stretch my legs, Noo-noo. Let's take a walk."

Noo-noo grinned at her, delighted by her restlessness, which so frequently ended up in taking walks. A minute later, Beatrice and Noo-noo set out.

The sun was starting to go down, but there was still plenty of light out. Noo-noo pulled at the leash, for once excited to walk more than sniff at things on the sides of the road. They passed by Felton's house and Beatrice's brow wrinkled at the memory of Felton calling them over and being kind to Will. A few moments later, she took a detour down the side road that led to the house where Rupert had been living. There was police tape on the front porch still and it looked like there was an investigator of some sort speaking with another police officer outside.

They walked for a while past neatly-trimmed lawns and neighbors who called out to say hi as they passed. Then Beatrice turned around and started heading back. She'd passed Rupert's house again, the property vacant now, and approached Edith's house when she heard someone calling out her name.

Chapter Seventeen

It was Edith. She beamed at her. "You're so good to get exercise. I really need to get more, myself. Maybe if I had a dog instead of a cat," she said ruefully.

"Oh, often it just helps me clear my head. Sometimes I'm not thinking about helping my heart or my blood pressure or my stress levels, or whatever else it's supposed to be good for. Sometimes I just need a change of scenery to be able to think better."

Edith stooped to pet Noo-noo. "That's so smart. See, that's what I should have been doing when all this started instead of baking cookies."

"Well, we all know what works for us to reduce stress. You weren't *eating* all the cookies, you were just baking them."

Edith said sadly, "I made some more and they're gone now. I did eat those." She cheered up momentarily. "Although I didn't make as many this time." She looked up at Beatrice. "Would you like to come in? I did feel so much better last time when you and Wyatt came by."

Beatrice could tell Edith was lonely. She didn't seem as close to others in Dappled Hills as she had to Felton and now Felton was gone. But Beatrice wasn't sure she was really in the mood to deal with Edith's fluffiness, either. It would probably put her right back in the spot she was in before she took the walk.

"But won't Coco be upset? I'd have to bring Noo-noo inside with me."

Edith blinked. "Noo-noo could stay out in the yard. I have a wonderful fence."

Beatrice shook her head. "She'd be upset, I'm afraid. Being in a different place with no one around? She'd probably cry. Also, it's starting to get later and I should get back home. I still haven't figured out what Wyatt and I are having for supper." She ruefully thought that she should have asked Meadow to add her to the list of people needing dinners.

Edith's eyes filled with tears and Beatrice looked at her with alarm. "Are you all right?"

Edith shook her head. "I just spend so much time *thinking*. And feeling bad. Oh, do come in. You can bring Noo-noo with you. Coco will jump up somewhere high if she doesn't like her. And Noo-noo is a really well-behaved dog. Here, I'll go find one of Coco's sturdier toys and some treats she can eat."

Beatrice sighed as Edith trotted off to prepare Coco for her canine guest. A text came in and she quickly checked it, hoping it would provide her with an excuse to leave. But it was only Miss Sissy, demanding to know when she was babysitting Will again. She reluctantly headed for the door, Noo-noo peering at her in confusion at the unusual deviation from the walk.

Edith's house was just as tidy as before, which led Beatrice to ask for a paper towel before she crossed the threshold. She wasn't sure if Noo-noo had dirty feet or not, but she didn't want to take any chances of leaving muddy pawprints. She might wipe her own shoes, while she was at it.

Edith was so pleased that Beatrice tried to rally. "Here is a toy for Noo-noo." She produced a stuffed doll modeled to look like a fish. "It's stuffed with catnip, but I suppose Noo-noo won't mind."

Noo-noo, who seemed to be a little uneasy, did start nosing the stuffed fish around and gnawing on a fin.

"And Noo-noo can have some of Coco's treats whenever she wants them. Coco wasn't as fond of these organic ones I picked up at the store. Do you think Noo-noo would like them?"

"Oh, this little dog likes everything. She's like a tummy with feet."

Edith beamed at her again. "And she can have some of Coco's water. It's a big bowl. Now for us!"

"Please, don't feel you need to get me anything. You fed Wyatt and me handsomely the last time we were here. It's nearly suppertime, too, and I shouldn't spoil my appetite." For what, Beatrice wasn't sure. It would likely, at this point, be grilled cheese sandwiches. She could hardly ask Wyatt to cook, considering the fact he'd been out of town at hospitals and retirement homes most of the day.

But Edith blithely ignored her protests and was digging in her fridge. "Here, I have some really good cheese here. I do like a good gouda, don't you? And I picked up some special crackers at the store. Milk again? Milk would go well with cheese."

Beatrice decided to give in gracefully. The last thing she wanted was for Edith to start dissolving into tears again. "That would be perfect. Can I give you a hand?"

"Oh, no, no. I've got it. It's my pleasure. Now that Felton's gone, I just haven't really had any guests here at all. It's made me feel very sad. It's a joy for me to be able to do some entertaining." She briskly put the cheese and crackers on a plate and cut the cheese into little squares.

Coco entered the kitchen looking very put-out. Noo-noo, used to friendly cats, curiously trotted over to nuzzle her. Coco's fur immediately stood on end and she gave Noo-noo a swipe on the nose, making the corgi yelp.

"Oh goodness!" said Edith. "Naughty Coco!"

Coco gave Edith a withering look and stalked away before hopping onto the back of an armchair to watch Noo-noo with an arch expression on her face.

Edith stooped in front of Noo-noo. "Are you okay, sweet-ie?"

Beatrice had already checked out Noo-noo's long nose. "She's fine. I think it was just a warning swat from Coco with no claws out. I can't really blame her, after all. This is her home and she isn't used to entertaining dogs."

"I suppose she's simply not used to other animals." Edith poured them both a glass of milk and set them on the table. She smiled in satisfaction at her handiwork. "All right, then! Let's dig in."

Beatrice realized it was good to have a snack. It had been a while since she'd last eaten. Edith had fallen silent as she ate, still giving Coco reproachful looks from time to time. Beatrice said, "Are you doing better, now? I know it was all such a shock. Time helps, though, doesn't it?"

Edith turned her attention back to Beatrice and nodded eagerly as if Beatrice had said something very original. "It does, doesn't it? I've been dreadfully upset about Felton and then really frightened after Rupert. But this afternoon I felt a good deal better."

Edith was quiet again and Beatrice again felt the urge to fill the silence. "I wonder what's going to happen to Felton's house and her things?" she said idly, almost to herself. "I suppose she would have left everything to Rupert. But with Rupert now gone, I wonder how that works?"

Edith said thoughtfully, "Perhaps Rupert had a will. I guess everything will go to whomever he put in his will." She paused. "I am glad that Felton's ring has been recovered. It gave me quite a turn when that was lost. She always wore it, you know. Always. Having it disappear like that really made everything that much worse."

Beatrice looked at her curiously. She knew Dappled Hills was a small town, but how would Edith have gotten news of the ring? It wasn't as if Devlin worked for her. Ramsay wasn't likely to have said anything.

"How did you hear about the ring being recovered?" asked Beatrice.

Edith looked flustered. "Oh, I don't know. I heard it from someone in town today, I'd expect."

Beatrice shook her head. "That's unlikely, actually. It's a detail that's being kept under wraps."

Edith flushed. "Well, I suppose it's just me being nosy. I was keeping an eye on Devlin while he was over at Rupert's, mostly because there was so much activity over there that I was trying to figure out if something had happened to Rupert. That must have been it."

Beatrice felt an icy shiver down her spine. She slowly said, "I don't think you'd have been able to see the ring from here, Edith. I mean, it's a large ring, but it's not *that* large."

Edith stared mutely at her.

"So how did you know about it?"

Edith's flush grew into angry splotches on her face and neck. "That's not a very nice thing to ask, Beatrice. It sounds like you don't trust me."

"It's just a point I'm confused about," said Beatrice slowly. And with that, she suddenly realized what it was that she'd been bothered by after she and Wyatt and been at Edith's house. "Something else confuses me, too. You mentioned the last time I visited here that you had never been in Rupert's house. But then later in the same conversation, you made a reference to the fact that the house 'barely had a stick of furniture in it.'"

Edith gave a dismissive snort and Noo-noo started eyeing her carefully. "Anyone knew that. Or maybe Felton told me the house was basically empty."

Noo-noo moved closer to Beatrice, staring between narrowed eyes at Edith as the dog registered her tone of voice.

"Did you put the ring in Devlin's truck? You'd have had plenty of opportunities to do that, wouldn't you? From here you have a perfect view of both Felton's house and Rupert's. And his truck isn't exactly quiet. You could have heard it coming, seen Devlin get his things out, and take a little stroll, casually putting the ring into the truck as you walked past."

Edith gave a short laugh. "The ring. That dumb ring."

Noo-noo edged on top of Beatrice's feet, in between the two women.

Beatrice felt herself become somehow very calm. "What do you mean? What makes the ring dumb?"

"People here have been laughing at me for years. Years! And I didn't even know. I believed everything that came out of Felton's mouth. But why wouldn't I? It just didn't occur to me that my best friend would be lying to me." Edith's eyes filled with furious tears.

"Edith, I have no idea what you're talking about," said Beatrice steadily. "I've never heard anyone laughing at you. Why would they? From what I hear, people are sorry that you've lost someone close to you."

Edith shook her head angrily. "No. No, that's not right. I'd repeat whatever Felton told me as if it were gospel. Even when Felton wasn't around, I'd keep telling her stories to everyone. Like an echo. Or her megaphone. That's probably why she liked having me around."

Beatrice flinched as Edith swooped down on the table, but she was only picking up the plates and taking them to the sink, apparently not able to stand untidiness for more than a minute. With shaking hands, she pulled out her phone. But she didn't have her reading glasses with her and only had a matter of seconds before Edith was sure to swoop down again for the milk glasses.

She went to her texting app and touched the first name, the most-recent person she'd texted, which was always Wyatt. The tiny keyboard that appeared was almost illegible, but she typed *help*.

Edith spun around and headed for the glasses. Beatrice smiled at her. "Could I have some more milk?"

Edith blinked at her. "Oh. Of course you can." She took her own glass away first to clean it and Beatrice added to her text *at Edith's* and then hit send and slid the phone back out of sight.

Edith picked up her glass and Beatrice said, "I don't know why I'm so thirsty. Could you leave the whole milk jug on the table so I can refill the glass myself? I must have walked longer today than I thought."

Edith looked doubtful at the mess that would ensue by having a milk container on the table. "I suppose so."

She filled Beatrice's glass and then set the jug on the table.

For a moment, Beatrice thought maybe she could quickly drink her milk, start talking about an innocuous subject like Coco and Noo-noo and the trials and tribulations of pet ownership, make her excuses, and hurry out the door. Her eyes flitted over to the door and Edith shook her head sadly.

"You can't leave, you know." Her voice sounded genuinely regretful.

Beatrice kept hers light. "Oh, believe me, I'd love to stay. I don't usually have such wonderful snacks. But Wyatt will be looking for me soon. I'll need to make us some supper." She stood up casually, but Edith shot up herself, a lot quicker than Beatrice imagined she could be.

In a cold voice she said, "You can't leave."

"Why is that, Edith?"

"Because now you know," she said simply. "It's what happens when people know. I can't get into trouble. It wouldn't be fair."

Beatrice listened desperately for the sound of Wyatt's car or for the buzz of an incoming text, but heard nothing. She glanced over at the milk jug, which she'd asked for in case she needed some sort of weapon. Edith followed her gaze and Beatrice duly poured herself some more milk, although she felt as though she might float away at this point. She didn't need to raise any suspicion.

Beatrice took a deep breath. She needed to stall her until Wyatt got here. And she wasn't altogether positive that he was back in Dappled Hills after having gone on his round of hospital and retirement home visits.

"Is that what happened to Rupert, then? Did he know?"

Edith nodded primly. "He did. He shouldn't have said anything, you know. He never did have any real feelings for his mother. He was probably glad she was gone. But he saw me go over there. He didn't have a job, you know. He's over at his house all the time. I guess I should have thought about that, but I didn't."

Beatrice said slowly, "So, Rupert saw you walk over to his mother's house. Even though you'd said you'd been here all day. He must have wondered why you hadn't been truthful about that."

Edith stared wordlessly at her.

"Felton was your best friend. What made you go over and push her down the stairs?"

Edith's voice was clipped. "Friends don't treat friends like that. She told me the ring was real. She told me she had a tiara. All those stories. And no one else was dumb enough to believe them. She must have thought I was so stupid. She didn't have any respect for me."

"I believed them, you know." Beatrice heard the roar of a car somewhere in the distance and her heart surged with relief. Surely, that had to be Wyatt. Or maybe Ramsay, if Wyatt had called him if he was still out of town at the hospital.

Edith stared dully at her. "No, you didn't. You're very smart. You had an important job in art, from what I remember." She tilted her head to one side. "What was it you did?"

"Art curation at a museum," answered Beatrice steadily. The car engine she heard was loud and the driving sounded erratic, but it was the sweetest sound she'd ever heard. "But that doesn't mean I didn't believe her. I'm afraid I just didn't *care*. I wasn't a good friend to Felton like you were. When she started telling her stories, I tried to find excuses for escaping the conversation. I never even looked at the ring very closely. If I had, I should have been able to tell it was a good piece of costume jewelry."

"With your job," nodded Edith. "Yes, that makes sense."

"I think there were many people like me," said Beatrice. "It wasn't as if the whole town thought you were the only one who believed Felton." She paused and Beatrice listened hard. The car outside had stopped outside the house, but now was revving its motor. Did it have car trouble or was something else going on?

Edith frowned at the car sounds and stood up, looking around her blankly. Beatrice hurried on. "So what happened with Felton?" Edith didn't seem inclined to talk, so Beatrice continued, "I'm guessing you finally spoke to someone who *knew* the ring was fake. The only person I know who was that convinced was Lucius Craft. I spoke with him myself and he told me he'd no doubt it was costume jewelry."

Edith looked at her sadly. "Lucius told me it wasn't real."

"Did he?" asked Beatrice, trying to keep her talking.

Edith nodded again. "I could tell he felt sorry for me when he did."

Beatrice took a deep breath. "So you went right over to talk to Felton, didn't you? Your feelings were hurt. And you thought you were the only person trusting enough in town to believe her. You were upstairs so maybe you demanded to see the tiara."

"She was always talking about it," said Edith. She picked up a wrought-iron fire poker from next to her fireplace and walked closer to Beatrice.

"You'd probably asked to see the tiara for ages and she'd always made excuses. But this time, you were insistent. And she couldn't deliver. You were hurt and furious and you acted out in a moment of passion." Beatrice reached out for the milk jug and felt its heaviness. She definitely didn't need to drink any more milk if it was going to remain an effective weapon. She listened out again for someone to burst into the house.

Edith held the fire poker aloft and her voice was cold. "Like I said, you're very smart." Noo-noo let out a low, warning growl and then started barking loudly, frantically, not liking the tone of Edith's voice or the menacing way she was approaching Beatrice.

"Shut her up," yelled Edith.

Beatrice stood up with the milk jug in hand and said nothing.

Noo-noo now interspersed the barking with some howling and was showing some teeth to Edith. Since Noo-noo had never bitten anything other than dog biscuits, Beatrice wasn't sure how far she'd take things, but she did seem very threatening.

Edith swiped toward Noo-noo with the fire poker and Beatrice struck her arm with the milk jug as hard as she could. Now Edith was howling, herself, and the fire poker clanged to the floor.

As Edith and Beatrice both lunged for it, there was suddenly a horrific crashing sound of metal meeting wood and other obstacles. The poker forgotten, Edith stared fearfully at her front door, which suddenly came crashing inwards.

A car's hood was barely visible under the wreckage of Edith's door, bits of bushes, and the front gate.

Chapter Eighteen

Beatrice retrieved the poker, clasping it firmly in one hand and the milk jug in the other as she ran to the car among the debris. Edith was frozen, staring in horror. Noo-noo stopped barking and trotted over toward the vehicle.

And suddenly, Miss Sissy appeared, looking fiercely determined and brandishing a pair of stainless-steel quilting shears, her hair completely out of its customary bun and flying around her shoulders as she whipped it from side to side, gauging where her enemies might leap out at her.

"Miss Sissy," gasped Beatrice weakly.

The old woman gave Beatrice a quick once-over as if evaluating her for injuries, then bobbed her head as if satisfied. She patted Noo-noo, glanced quickly over her, too. Then she leveled her narrowed eyes at Edith.

Beatrice could hear the faint sound of sirens.

Edith hissed at Miss Sissy. "My gate! My house!"

The old woman waved the scissors wildly at her.

"You wouldn't," said Edith coldly.

Beatrice said, "Oh, that's the thing about Miss Sissy. She's completely unpredictable."

Miss Sissy snarled at Edith. Noo-noo did the same.

Edith backed away.

The sirens were now right on top of them and moments later, policemen, firemen, and paramedics rushed inside.

At first, it appeared the police were unsure whom to arrest first. Miss Sissy appeared, at the moment, to be the dangerous one. But Beatrice redirected them to Edith, who was now flustered, confused, and seemingly completely benign.

Wyatt was there shortly afterward, rushing straight to her to give her a hug.

"I'm so sorry I wasn't here," he said into her hair.

Beatrice was still holding herself together by a thread, so said briskly, "It wasn't your fault. And everything worked out fine."

Ramsay and another officer had already led Edith out to a police cruiser. He came back in the house, shaking his head at the damage.

"So, Miss Sissy, you *deliberately* ran the car into the house, is that right?"

Miss Sissy muttered with great satisfaction to the affirmative.

Ramsay rubbed his forehead. "That's because you were trying to help Beatrice?"

Miss Sissy nodded, looking at him scornfully for not immediately grasping the point.

"How did you know she was in trouble?" asked Ramsay, slowly.

Miss Sissy's gaze shifted to me and I said, "I have something to do with that. While Edith was distracted, I fumbled around with my phone and texted the top number from my most recent messages. I thought it would be Wyatt, but I'd forgotten Miss Sissy had texted me a little while ago."

"Needed help," said Miss Sissy emphatically.

"I sure did," agreed Beatrice.

"And Noo-noo," added Miss Sissy.

Ramsay glanced down at Noo-noo, who was still lying protectively on Beatrice's feet.

"Noo-noo went ballistic," said Beatrice. "She found Edith's body language and tone very threatening."

"And rightly so," said Ramsay with a sigh. He took his notebook out. "Okay. Miss Sissy, let me get a brief statement from you first and then I can have one of the guys drive you back home. I have the feeling that car of yours might need to go in the shop."

Miss Sissy glowered at him and Ramsay said, "Just a few words to explain what happened and why you did what you did."

"She was in trouble. Dog barked. Ran car into house." Miss Sissy shrugged, looking at Ramsay as if anyone with any sense at all should have been able to see what happened.

Ramsay sighed and opened his mouth as if considering pushing for more information, but then shrugged. "All right, then. Let's get you back home."

Miss Sissy stomped off with Ramsay scampering to keep up.

Wyatt squeezed Beatrice's hand and she gave a hoarse chuckle. "Ramsay was right to give up with that line of questioning. I should be able to fill him in better."

"The most important thing is that you're okay. I've called Piper and filled her in so she didn't end up hearing about this from someone else."

Beatrice said, "Thanks."

Ramsay came back over and Wyatt said, "Could we take Beatrice somewhere else?"

Noo-noo looked imploringly at Ramsay as Coco's tail swished menacingly at the group.

"You mean away from the scene of an attempted murder? Absolutely." He looked at Coco and sighed. "We'll have to find a good home for the kitty. That's all Edith is talking about right now is the cat. I'm pretty sure Miz Swanson will take in another furry lodger. She already has seven, but is always on the lookout for more. And she takes great care of them. I don't know how she has as many animals as she does when her house is as clean as a whistle."

They carefully navigated around Miss Sissy's wrecked Lincoln and Ramsay followed as Wyatt drove Beatrice and Noo-noo home.

Beatrice plopped down on the sofa. Wyatt poured Beatrice a glass of white wine and made coffee for Ramsay.

Ramsay sat across from Beatrice and pulled out his notebook. "Let's see. Where to start? How about with Noo-noo? What set her off?"

Beatrice took a good-sized sip of her wine. "She seemed to be picking up on both my unease and Edith's odd manner."

Ramsay nodded, jotting down notes. "Edith was acting threatening?"

"She certainly *became* that way. But she started off just sort of menacing."

Wyatt handed Ramsay his coffee and joined them.

"What set her off?" Ramsay took a sip of his coffee.

Beatrice said dryly, "Well, for one, she knew about the ring being in Devlin's truck. She realized I was on to her at that point. Aside from that, she was very agitated about Felton's lies."

Ramsay nodded. "The state police have been grilling her. I spoke to them on the phone on the way over here. She's been very animated whenever the topic of the jewelry comes up."

"Edith seemed to think everyone in Dappled Hills knew the truth except her. As if she was the only person in town who was a fervent Felton-believer. She felt she looked foolish and silly and that made her upset. It sounded like she was confronting Felton about the jewelry and then just lashed out at her on the stairs."

"Which sounds as if she might not even have intended on killing Felton. But then we get into Rupert's death and it's a bit murkier," said Ramsay.

"Rupert figured out Edith was responsible for his mother's death. And, as we know, he was pretty low on funds. He decided to try to make Edith pay up in exchange for not telling the police he'd spotted her over at his mother's house," said Beatrice.

Ramsay nodded. "Those houses all overlook each other. It would have been easy enough for him to see her coming or going from Felton's house."

Beatrice said, "Rupert had been away from Dappled Hills long enough that he wouldn't have known Edith didn't have any money. Maybe she stalled him, too, to give herself time to figure out what she wanted to do. Maybe she told him she *would* pay him. Then she came back the following day and caught Rupert off-guard."

"That must have been easy enough to do," said Wyatt. "Edith didn't look dangerous."

Beatrice said, "Exactly. Thankfully, I realized exactly how dangerous she was before it was too late. I picked up a milk container and hit Edith's arm as she was swinging a fire poker around."

"I'm a little confused how Miss Sissy came barreling into the house." Ramsay tapped his pen against his notepad.

"I thought I was texting Wyatt, forgetting Miss Sissy had texted me last. She got the message and drove over. Plus, I got the impression she wasn't at all fond of Edith."

Ramsay nodded. "That's the case, for sure. I heard her hissing at her just last week. And Edith was just sweeping her front walk, minding her own business."

Beatrice said, "So she didn't need a lot of justification. But I guess she paused outside the house long enough to hear Noo-noo barking. She mentioned it specifically."

Noo-noo, who'd been lying on her back and snoring with gusto, opened her eyes at the sound of her name before quickly falling back to sleep.

"I guess Miss Sissy knew Edith didn't have a dog," said Ramsay.

"And she plowed right into the house," said Beatrice.

Ramsay shook his head. "And all because Edith felt foolish for believing Felton." Ramsay snapped his fingers. "Before I forget, I wanted to give you an update on Haskell. I know y'all are both concerned about him and Betty is such an involved member of the church."

Beatrice frowned. "Don't tell me anything bad happened. I saw the direction things were going in when he was talking with you in the church office." She glanced over at Wyatt, "I didn't even have a chance to tell you about it today. Ramsay was asking Haskell questions about where he was when Rupert was murdered and Haskell was really pushing back. But he ended up having an alibi."

Ramsay said, "Yeah, things weren't looking so good at the church. That must have been a real low point for the kid. I've spoken with him before at church and he was always very polite. Seemed like a completely different person during that conversation. I'd also heard some rumors he was hanging out with a rough crowd of kids and they had gotten him hooked on drugs."

"Oh no," said Wyatt under his breath.

"Anyway, Betty gave me an update later today—I think because she was so grateful we'd pressured Haskell to give us the alibi. It seems when he left the church on his bike, he went to see his new friend. His alibi, actually, Dawn Playford."

Beatrice said, "I hope she's a better influence than the other kids he'd been hanging around."

Ramsay nodded. "Seems she is. He was apparently really strung out and told her about what happened. He was itchy to head off to Lenoir and hook up with his new friends over there and get his hands on some more drugs to help him forget what had happened. She told him he was getting hooked and apparently she'd had a cousin or close friend who'd overdosed. Dawn persuaded him to go home instead and tell his mom that he needed help."

Wyatt's face was relieved. Beatrice said, "I'm so glad."

Ramsay said, "Like I said, she gave me a call both to update me and to find out if I could recommend a good rehab place for Haskell to kick his habit. She's called them up, they had a space, and she's on her way there now with Haskell."

Beatrice smiled at him. "That's fabulous news. Dawn sounds like she's really good for him."

Ramsay said wryly, "Well, sometimes girlfriends can be pretty influential at that age."

The door swung open and Piper was standing there with little Will. Noo-noo bounded up joyfully to greet them as Piper hurried forward and gave her mother a fierce hug as Ramsay gingerly took Will out of her arms to free them.

"I'm *so glad* you're okay," whispered Piper.

"Me too," said Beatrice, hugging her back.

"There's someone else glad you're okay," said Piper, pulling back with a grin. "I saw Meadow's car pulling in just as soon as I made it to the door."

As if in response to her words, Meadow burst through the door, breathless, gaze roaming around the room until it locked on Beatrice. She dove at her and propelled her to the sofa.

"Why aren't you sitting down?" she fussed.

"I was just greeting Piper and Will. And you," said Beatrice mildly.

"Well don't! Just sit down and we'll come to you. It's the least we can do." She turned and glowered at Ramsay, who was 'flying' the baby around like a little airplane as Will gave deep chuckles. "What are you doing to our grandchild?"

Ramsay said, "He's having a blast! Look how much fun he's having."

Meadow ignored him completely, plucking Will out of his arms and bustling back over to Beatrice to plop the baby into her lap.

"Here. If anyone needs a cuddle, Beatrice does," she said.

Beatrice was so flabbergasted at Meadow's unheard-of generosity with Will that she opened her mouth before shutting it wordlessly again.

The baby gave her a gummy grin before sticking his finger in his mouth and looking thoughtfully at her. Beatrice lay her cheek on the top of his fuzzy hair and breathed in his baby scent.

Meadow put her hands on her hips and turned to Ramsay. "Now do I understand correctly that Miss Sissy saved the day? I'm hearing all sorts of crazy rumors in town."

Ramsay said, "I think Beatrice was probably able to get herself out of the jam with the milk jug she said she was swinging, but from what I understand, Miss Sissy helped a lot."

Wyatt chuckled. "She provided quite a distraction."

Meadow said, "The distraction was what I saw on the way over here. Miss Sissy's Lincoln in Edith's living room. It's amazing she didn't run over you on the way in."

Beatrice said dryly, "I'm not sure she put that much thought and planning into it."

Meadow heaved a sigh. "Well, that's that, then. I'm going to have to keep Miss Sissy on the meal list for the conceivable future. As a thank you, you know."

Ramsay perked up at the mention of the meal list. It seemed he would be having tasty, planned suppers for a while.

Piper said with a smile, "Those meals are really a life-saver. I know Miss Sissy will appreciate them, too."

Ramsay said, "On that note, I'm going to head out. I need to help the state police with Edith's interview."

Meadow said, "I'll leave y'all, too, now that I've seen with my own eyes that you're all right. And next time, Beatrice, I plan on helping you get to the bottom of things. I've been so caught up with being a new grandma that I just didn't jump in like I usually do. I feel terrible about not being there with you when you were facing off against Edith."

"Let's hope there *isn't* a next time," said Beatrice wryly. "And I'm glad you didn't put yourself in any danger, believe me."

Meadow snapped her fingers. "Wait. I almost forgot that I picked up supper for you and Wyatt after I heard what was going on. I'd have cooked something myself, but that food is all spoken for tonight." She ran back out to her car and returned with a large foil casserole dish. "I picked up lasagna to go from the Italian place downtown. I thought some comfort food might be in order."

Beatrice's stomach growled on cue as the aroma of the lasagna wafted her way. She patted it ruefully. "Thanks, Meadow. I think it's about time to eat."

Meadow grinned at her and said, "I'll catch up with you tomorrow." She left just as quickly as she'd arrived.

Piper said, "Mama, I think I should leave you to get some rest now, too. Is that okay? I know you're getting a cuddle in."

Beatrice gave the baby one final gentle hug and then lifted him back up to Piper. "He's looking a little sleepy, too. No point in having him fall asleep over here and then waking him back up again to go home."

A few minutes later, the house was quiet. Wyatt fixed them both a hearty portion of the lasagna, which ended up being as tasty as it smelled. He put on some relaxing jazz music to play and got them both a glass of wine (Beatrice's second).

Beatrice gave him a grateful look. "Thanks for making this evening relaxing for me. I think I'll follow this up with a warm bath and then roll myself into the bed."

Which is exactly what happened. With Noo-noo along, since she apparently felt it was now her appointed duty to keep a close eye on Beatrice at all times.

About the Author:

Elizabeth writes the Southern Quilting mysteries and Memphis Barbeque mysteries for Penguin Random House and the Myrtle Clover series for Midnight Ink and independently. She blogs at ElizabethSpannCraig.com/blog, named by Writer's Digest as one of the 101 Best Websites for Writers. Elizabeth makes her home in Matthews, North Carolina, with her husband. She's the mother of two.

Sign up for Elizabeth's free newsletter to stay updated on releases:

https://bit.ly/2xZUXqO

This and That

I love hearing from my readers. You can find me on Facebook as Elizabeth Spann Craig Author, on Twitter as elizabethscraig, on my website at elizabethspanncraig.com, and by email at elizabethspanncraig@gmail.com.

Thanks so much for reading my book...I appreciate it. If you enjoyed the story, would you please leave a short review on the site where you purchased it? Just a few words would be great. Not only do I feel encouraged reading them, but they also help other readers discover my books. Thank you!

Did you know my books are available in print and ebook formats? Most of the Myrtle Clover series is available in audio and some of the Southern Quilting mysteries are. Find the audiobooks here.

I have Myrtle Clover tote bags, charms, magnets, and other goodies at my Café Press shop: https://www.cafepress.com/cozymystery

If you'd like an autographed book for yourself or a friend, please visit my Etsy page.

I'd also like to thank some folks who helped me put this book together. Thanks to my cover designer, Karri Klawiter, for her awesome covers. Thanks to my editor, Judy Beatty for her help. Thanks to beta readers Amanda Arrieta and Dan Harris for all of their helpful suggestions and careful reading. Thanks to Chris Stewart for her support! Thanks to my ARC readers for helping to spread the word. Thanks, as always, to my family and readers.

Other Works by Elizabeth:

Myrtle Clover Series in Order (be sure to look for the Myrtle series in audio, ebook, and print):

Pretty is as Pretty Dies

Progressive Dinner Deadly

A Dyeing Shame

A Body in the Backyard

Death at a Drop-In

A Body at Book Club

Death Pays a Visit

A Body at Bunco

Murder on Opening Night

Cruising for Murder

Cooking is Murder

A Body in the Trunk

Cleaning is Murder

Edit to Death

Hushed Up

A Body in the Attic (2020)

Southern Quilting Mysteries in Order:

Quilt or Innocence

Knot What it Seams
Quilt Trip
Shear Trouble
Tying the Knot
Patch of Trouble
Fall to Pieces
Rest in Pieces
On Pins and Needles
Fit to be Tied
Embroidering the Truth (2020)

THE VILLAGE LIBRARY Mysteries in Order (Debuting 2019):
Checked Out
Overdue
Borrowed Time (2020)
Memphis Barbeque Mysteries in Order (Written as Riley Adams):
Delicious and Suspicious
Finger Lickin' Dead
Hickory Smoked Homicide
Rubbed Out
And a standalone "cozy zombie" novel: Race to Refuge, written as Liz Craig